Mortimer Dormer Leggett

A Dream of a Modest Prophet

Mortimer Dormer Leggett

A Dream of a Modest Prophet

ISBN/EAN: 9783337047061

Printed in Europe, USA, Canada, Australia, Japan

Cover: Foto ©Andreas Hilbeck / pixelio.de

More available books at **www.hansebooks.com**

A DREAM

OF

A MODEST PROPHET.

BY

M. D. LEGGETT.

———

PHILADELPHIA:
J. B. LIPPINCOTT COMPANY.
1890.

A DREAM

A MODEST PROPHET.

PRELUDE.

IT is now generally conceded by all well-informed people that our Solar System had a nebular genesis,—that our system of worlds, consisting of the Sun and the surrounding planets, was at one time in the progress of creation or evolution a great nebulous mass of sublimated matter, in form of vapor or gas. This idea was first dimly suggested, perhaps by Plato, about four hundred years before Christ, but more fully developed by Laplace, about the beginning of the present century, and very nearly or quite demonstrated by later scientists. The theory, briefly stated, is that long anterior to the measure of time on earth, many millions of years before, the whole Solar System was a gaseous mass, without form and void. The force of gravitation, acting upon this mass, caused the

3

particles to be attracted towards its centre. The
various currents natural to the fluid or gaseous
mass of matter would finally be overcome by
the strongest current, and this was evidently
from the west to the east, so that the whole
mass partook of this motion, which gave it a
revolution in that direction on a common axis.
This motion caused a flattening at the poles and
a bulging on the equatorial line. As this mass
continued to contract, the velocity of rotation
would increase, which would lead to separation
of rings from the equator, where the centrif-
ugal force was greatest. These rings would
break into fragments, some larger and some
smaller. As these fragments would all be
moving in the same path in space, the largest
would gradually, by its superior attraction, ac-
celerate the motion of the fragments behind
it, and retard that of those before it, so that
in time they would come together, forming a
planet. It is supposed that in this way all the
planets, moons, Saturn's rings, etc., were formed.
After the separation of these rings, and the collection of their material into one body, such
material was still nebular, and acted upon by
the same laws as the original mass, and the
process of solidification continued.

If Neptune is our outer planet, or the one
furthest from the Sun, then by this theory it is

the oldest planet,—the first-born of the Solar
family.   Uranus is next, then Saturn, Jupiter,
the Asteroids, Mars, Earth, Venus, and the
youngest, Mercury.

The length of time intervening between these
successive separations, or planetary births, is,
of course, all a matter of speculation.   We
simply know these periods must have been very
long.

If this theory of the creation of the heavens
and the earth be correct, then we must conclude
that in substance the planets are all the same as
the earth, and much like it, and subject to the
same natural laws.   But the further the planet
is from the Sun the rarer will be its substance,
and the less heat will it get from the Sun.
Hence it is doubtful whether the density and
temperature of the outer planets render them
inhabitable for man.

But Mars being so near the Earth, its conditions cannot be greatly different, and it is
reasonably certain that it is inhabited by beings
much like ourselves, for the same evolutionary
laws have operated there as here, and have had
like material to work upon.   And as Mars is
probably many millions of years older than the
Earth, it has, undoubtedly, been inhabited much
longer.   Being further from the Sun, it solidi-
fied more slowly than the Earth did, yet it is

1*

reasonable to suppose that it was inhabited by rational beings thousands of years before the Earth was.

The people of Mars are our nearest older neighbors. What is their condition? Have they advanced beyond us in civilization? They have lived on their planet much longer than we have on ours. If they are equally teachable, they must have learned more. If they had the means of doing so, and the disposition, I wonder if they could not, from their experience, greatly enlighten our statesmen and our students of sociology on questions now vexing us. Possibly they have already been able to construct telescopes of sufficient power to enable them to see us and know much that we are doing. If we had telescopes of equal power, communication might be had by way of signals, out of which would spring a language intelligible to both; then we could exchange thoughts, experiences, and histories. From such an exchange we, of course, would be the gainers, provided their progress, from the beginning, has been as rapid as ours, because the race there has existed longer. Perhaps in their past, at some time, they were where we are now. If so, and if we could gain access to their libraries and in their ancient histories find the present status of our civilization, how prophetic their subsequent history would be of what lies before us! In the light of such subsequent history, how clearly we might read our way out of many serious questions that now confront us in our march of civilization, and thus, profiting by their experience, we might progress in a few hundred years over what required thousands of years with them. They might quickly convey to us what they have slowly learned, and thus we might attain with a bound what has cost them long cycles of blunderings and sufferings in the slow progress of learning by experience.

CHAPTER I.

THE preceding was written with no definite object in view, except to follow a habit, long since established, of putting on paper any novel trains of thought, afterwards to be worked into an essay or thrown into the trash-basket, as mood might suggest. The act of writing puts a thought into expressible form, and tends to fix it in the mind. After writing, I found my mind in a thoughtful and somewhat speculative mood, and possessed of an uncontrollable desire to know more of the people of Mars. This feeling finally became so strong as to suspend consciousness of my surroundings. I awoke to consciousness on the planet Mars. How or when I got there I do not know; but my heart's desire was realized,—I was there. I was astonished and bewildered by all I saw.

Mars is much smaller than the Earth, but its population is so dense that it has about twice as many people. Its days have about the same length as ours, but its seasons are much longer, the year being six hundred and eighty-seven days. Its surface is composed of land and water in about the same proportion as the Earth. What most impressed me at first, and all the time, was the people, even before I had learned their language, so as to hold any conversation with them. Almost every one I saw seemed to be in robust health and in a happy and contented state of mind. The entire absence of large cities was very noticeable. The people seemed to be quite evenly distributed over the land surface of the planet, the density of population being affected only by the comparative fertility of the soil or desirable mineral deposits. Educational institutions seemed plentiful everywhere, and to be well patronized, while penal institutions and almshouses were very few. All seemed ambitious and industrious, yet there was none of the hurry and scramble to which I had so long been accustomed. Their manners were easy and graceful, gentility was universal, salutations were universally exchanged when people met, whether acquainted or not, and they addressed each other in language of deference and respect, but entirely without regard to rank.

At first the ladies did not impress me as possessed of much beauty. The frail, delicate, wasp-like forms to which we are so accustomed here, where nature's forms are compressed out of shape to conform to artificial standards of æsthetics, are not to be found there. I very soon, however, became not only reconciled to, but a great admirer of, their style of beauty, and almost every woman was really beautiful. No one looked coarse or gross. Their wonderful temperance in eating and drinking, and the absence of excessive excitement of every kind, make health universal. Obesity is not known, neither is excessive leanness. All are robust and healthy. The blood is pure, the complexion wonderfully clear and roseate. Their happy and contented life for many generations past has left its hereditary impress on the features in lines of beauty on the faces of both women and men. The laws of health seem to be well understood and religiously observed. Such has been the case for more than a thousand years; hence there are no blood-taints, no transmitted diseases. Every one inherits a good constitution, physical, intellectual, and moral; and from earliest infancy they are trained to habits of strict obedience to the laws of health of these three elements of their natures.

Another thing that attracted my special attention was the fact that there was but one language spoken on the planet. Whatever part of the planet the people came from, they readily conversed with and understood each other, and the same appearance and habits seemed to prevail everywhere. All seemed well informed, and all were religious. Their religion did not seem to be so much a *doctrine* as a *life*.

They professed little, but practised much. Their religion controlled them in all they did. It seemed to be born in them, and had a controlling influence from the beginning of life. There appeared to be no sectarian strife whatever; in fact, I saw no indication of there being any sects. They had places and societies for worship, but I saw nothing to indicate any divisions on doctrinal lines. Places of worship were so distributed and located as to best accommodate the worshippers. I do not mean that they all thought just alike on religious questions, for evidently they did not. On what constituted a proper religious life there were no differences, so that persons entertaining different views on matters having no bearing on practical life worshipped together, and yet all could engage in a friendly discussion of non-essentials. Their places of worship were neat, convenient, and comfortable, but never gaudy or expensive. Their forms of worship were very simple and direct. They appeared to have but little use for priests or potentates. Their religion was a personal religion. Each individual recognized his personal and direct responsibility to God for what he was and what he did. There seemed to be no effort or desire to enforce uniformity of belief or ritual. The *individual* is acknowledged as the unit of society, and individualism is encouraged and taught everywhere. Their whole system of religion and education seems to aim to make each individual strong in himself, self-reliant, self-controlled, conscious of personal independence, and acknowledging his personal responsibility only to God and to the laws and regulations necessary in a well-ordered state.

Courts of justice seemed to have but little to do. It was rarely in the lifetime of a judge that he would have a single criminal case before him. And the civil cases were remarkable for the entire absence of acrimony and unkind feelings exhibited in them. Parties came into court when there was an honest, conscientious difference of opinion, which both desired should be adjusted and settled. I saw no implements of war, no war-vessels, and no military fortifications or other defences, yet in some places I saw evidences of these having existed in the distant past. Large cities with protective walls and fortified positions there had been, but all had gone to decay, and their material had been converted to other uses,—"beaten into plough-shares and pruning-hooks."

Property was much more evenly distributed

than here. There seemed to be no very rich
and no very poor people, but all seemed to have
enough, and therewith to be content. Very
few were dependent on others for support, but
each endeavored, by honest labor, to produce
the full equivalent of what he or she consumed.
Their dress and their simple food and drink
were so inexpensive that ordinary industry was
sufficient to supply abundantly all necessary
wants, and there appeared no disposition to
increase these wants by any luxurious or expensive habits. In fact, any tendencies towards
such habits met with universal disapproval and
were very unpopular. There was nothing like
communism anywhere perceptible. Property,
beyond what was necessary for plain, healthful
living, was not desirable, for it gave no more
influence and no better social position, and consequently would only increase one's cares and
responsibilities, with no increased advantages.
Social position was won only by intelligence
and usefulness, while the possession of unneeded
wealth so distracted the attention as to hinder
one in attaining these desirable ends. The in-
vention of labor-saving machinery was much
encouraged, and the inventors of such were
greatly honored. Useful and practical inventions had been carried to far greater perfection
than with us. Nearly all fatiguing labor was

2

done with machinery,—so that persons only needed to supervise the machines,—and thereby the hours of labor were much reduced, and the people were hopefully looking forward to the time when machines would be so perfected as to allow the operators to supervise them with but little interruption of reading and study. They have nothing corresponding to our saloons, or gambling-houses, or club-halls, etc. Relief from labor is sought only for the purpose of having more time for personal improvement. But the sense of justice is too strong to permit one to get this time by employing others to do his individual work.

In dress they had a simple, inexpensive, but neat and graceful costume, common to all the people everywhere. These costumes for the men and women differed but slightly, sufficiently, however, easily to distinguish the sexes.

These costumes being universal, there was no chasing or studying of fashion, and no remodelling of garments; consequently all could and did dress well. A garment was in fashion until worn out. So, while there was no lack of comfort as to food and clothing, and no lack of neatness or even of elegance, yet the expense of living seemed to be reduced to the minimum.

They were all scrupulously clean. Cleanliness was nearer than "*next* to godliness :" it seemed to be a part of it. The daily bath was universal, so that the disease, with us known as "a cold," was almost unknown. "A cold," we understand here, fits the system for nearly all other forms of disease; consequently most of our diseases begin with colds. On Mars their simple and regular habits of eating and drinking, and dressing, and bathing, protect them fully from "colds." Sickness is scarcely known. Their longevity is remarkable, for men are in the full vigor of manhood at the age of one hundred.

Of course, when I found myself on Mars, I was very awkwardly situated. I was transported to that strange land, how and when .I do not know. I had made no preparations for the trip. I had "neither purse nor scrip," and no "letter of credit." I was a stranger, and a strange stranger, in a strange land. I could not understand a word of their language, nor they a word of mine. Yet into the first house I entered I was most heartily welcomed. By turning my pockets inside out and shaking them, I made them understand my poverty. The inmates of the house seemed at once to comprehend the situation. Though filled with wondering astonishment at my strange appearance, they, by kindly attention and appropriate gestures, made me feel that their home was my home and their possessions were mine. Everywhere on the planet I received the same cordial treatment.

I began to doubt my senses, my identity, and doubt as to where I really was. I began to think I had died on earth and, by some undeserved favor, had gone to heaven, for I had never dreamed of such people out of heaven. I could see no "great white throne," nor did I discover that all the people were singing psalms, nor did I hear the clangor of horns about which I had heard so much, and of which I had some dread. I was never fond of too much music, and it never took a great deal to be too much. But the people seemed good enough, pure enough, and happy enough to be the inhabitants of heaven. They were heavenly in disposition, and heavenly in conduct. But I saw that I had my earthly body and my earthly garments, and I was sure that neither "body nor boots" go to heaven. So I concluded that I was with people like myself, except that they were almost infinitely nearer perfection.

Whenever I went out from the home where I first stopped, they would give me a card on which they would write, in substance, "He is from Earth. Show him kindness and attention." Such I later found to be the true translation of this card. It served well its purpose, for the people seemed to vie with each other in their efforts to do me favors.

When I commenced studying their language, I could not readily see how I was to pay teachers, buy necessary books, etc. But here again every want was more than supplied, without money and without price. The inscription on my card was made to read, "He is from Earth, studying our language. Help him." This card made every man, woman, and child I met my teacher,—and such delightful teachers as they were! They thoroughly understand what they want to teach, and they know exactly how to teach it. I afterwards learned that every child is carefully instructed in the art of teaching, and parents practise this art, wisely and well, in the training of their own children. I had become somewhat familiar with the English, French, and German languages, and in my younger days knew something of Latin and Greek, and I had heard many other languages spoken; but the language of Mars was radically different from any I had ever read or heard. I was therefore expecting great difficulty in learning to speak and read this new and singular language. The reader may judge of my happy surprise when I found it very easy to acquire. In the short space of three months

b 2*

(our time) I could speak it with considerable fluency, and within six months I could read and write it with great satisfaction. Their written and printed language is entirely phonetic; so I had only to learn the elementary sounds, and the characters or letters representing those sounds, when I could read easily any of their printed books.

Before learning their language I could acquire knowledge only through my eyes, and, for want of explanations, I only understood a small fraction of what I saw. Now my ears were opened, and my tongue was loosened, and I rapidly gained a knowledge of my surroundings. I had all along been exceedingly anxious to learn to read, so as to look into their libraries, hoping that there I might discover the route by which these people had reached their high civilization and almost perfect manhood and womanhood. So I labored hard, in season and out of season, and had freely all the help I could possibly use. In every house there was a good library, and in every neighborhood a large public library of books for consultation and reference, but these were not allowed to be taken from the library buildings. The studious habits and the intelligence of the people may be judged by their use of these great libraries. Almost the whole population, excepting young children, will be found in them during some portions of nearly every day.

Their language is peculiar in other respects besides being phonetic. They use fewer words to express the same idea than we do. Their style is peculiarly direct and pungent. Many of their words express what would require a clause or sentence with us.

They have another peculiarity. When I first began to read their books, particularly those of a philosophical character, their style seemed very dogmatic. Their assertions seemed to be without the support of any legitimate process of reasoning, but, as I extended my studies, I found this was true only in appearance, as the reasoning could always be read between the lines. To avoid multiplying words and lumbering sentences, they seem to have cultivated the habit of stating the results of their reasonings in such direct and logical order as to make the process at once inferable and apparent.

CHAPTER II.

These libraries contained very interesting revelations to me. The laws of evolution had operated there as here. Man has gone through the same stages of development there as here. The history of our race here up to the present time is described more perfectly in their books than in any we have. About three thousand years ago the people of Mars were in the same condition our people are in to-day, and had the same unsolved problems confronting them. They had many nations and many tongues. Their governments differed widely from each other, and their interests, as they then considered them, conflicted with each other. Hence there were strifes, and bloodshed, and wars of one nation against another.

In religious sentiments they were much more divided than on political questions. Their religion consisted more in codes of belief, in creeds, than in life and practice. I found that in the early historic age of the church they had an organization exactly resembling our ancient Jewish church, with its teachers and prophets, its priests and doctors, its temples and altars and sacrifices. Their Egypt and Greece and Rome and Constantinople had existed, had had their day, left their impress, and passed into oblivion.

When the times were ripe, a Christ had appeared there as here, and took to them the same message from the Father, the same gospel that our Christ brought to us. He found there, as our Christ found here, the people buried in corruption everywhere. Even in the Jewish church all practical religion was lost in forms, and ceremonies, and burnt-offerings, and blood-sacrifices. Religion was objective, and never subjective. It consisted in the practice of rites and ceremonies, and not in personal character. The teachings of their Christ, as of ours, consisted in a subjective religion,—a religion of the heart, the source of thought and action; a religion of love, that reached out to strangers and even to enemies, that returned good for evil, that recognized all men as brethren; a religion of justice, that metes out to every one his own, and that leads one to do unto others as he would that others should do unto him. He taught that God was not merely the personification of justice, power, and authority, heard only in thunders and lightnings, in earthquakes and tornadoes, in famines and pestilences; but that he was also a Father, possessed in an infinite degree of all the attributes of a father, endowed with infinite love and mercy and compassion, with an ear open to penitence, and waiting in mercy to forgive.

Their Christ, like ours, was crucified, dead, and buried. His disciples, like the disciples of our Christ, only partially understood their Master, only partially comprehended his character and mission. They were of the people we call Jews, had been reared and educated in the Jewish church, and could not fully rid themselves of certain Jewish teachings which were in conflict with the whole spirit of Christ's teachings, and, consequently, they carried over much of this early education into the Christian church, and for two thousand years Christianity was made to suffer by being loaded down by Judaism to an extent not justified by the teachings of Christ. Yet, for a little over three hundred years, Christianity was a life-principle, a heart-religion, and, its votaries being persecuted by the civil and military powers, it was maintained in its purity, substantially as taught by Christ. But a little over three hundred years after the crucifixion of Christ, a ruler, answering exactly to our Emperor Constantine, adopted Christianity as the state religion. Then, at once, persecution ceased, and priests and bishops of the

Christian church began to fawn on power, and in return obtained authority to enforce their ecclesiastical decrees. This power soon corrupted the lives of church officials, and consequently their religion. They began to add to the teachings of Christ, and what they added was not always in accord with what Christ taught. They also began to omit much that was essential in Christianity, as promulgated by Christ. Their Christian church, for the first nineteen hundred years of its existence, was almost literally the same as ours up to this time. They passed the point where we now are somewhat more than three thousand years ago.

The adoption of Christianity as the state religion opened their courts of state to the Christian bishops and priests; but this does not mean that members of the court practised any Christian self-denial, or abstained from any of the then court pleasures. The priesthood lowered its standard of Christian life to adapt it to court life. To maintain such lives and still remain Christian required that the standard of Christianity must also be lowered. The Christian religion must become more pliable and indulgent, so the doctrine of substitution was devised and added to Christian doctrine. This doctrine meant that personal character had but little to do with salvation,—that when man had lived as perfectly as he knew how, and to the fullest extent in his power followed in the footsteps of his Saviour, still he fell far short of what was demanded. To meet this demand they held that the righteousness of Christ must be set to man's credit, so that man was to be saved, not because he had any merit, but because of the merit of Christ. If man believed in Christ, and had faith that Christ's merit would at last be placed to his credit, without regard to his own personal character, such faith would secure him everlasting life.

This doctrine took the heart and vitality of Christ's teachings out of Christianity, and thereby left a Christless Christianity, well fitted for a court religion. The state was not Christianized so much as Christianity was secularized.

The common people in the Christian church were slow to adopt this innovation, but the priesthood, having free access to court, rapidly gained civil as well as ecclesiastical power. Synods were called, wherein were assembled the priests and bishops of nearly all the Christian churches, by the quasi-authority of the state. These synods fully adopted this and other innovations, and declared their non-acceptance heresy.

There was a series of rulers there, known as the Christian emperors, but their modern historians give these emperors little credit for their Christianity. They charge them with nominally adopting Christianity merely to strengthen their hold upon the government among the people and to get the benefit of Christian enthusiasm in their armies. They tried, as far as possible, to harmonize Christianity with the surrounding paganism, and thus, by the aid of a corrupted, power-seeking priesthood, they did much more to paganize Christianity than to Christianize paganism.

All idol-worshipping tribes there, as here, in olden times, and also their people corresponding to our Jews, had for many ages been familiar with the idea of placating the wrath of their gods by sacrifices. In early historic times parents sacrificed their children, and in times of public calamities the rulers levied upon the adult populations for public sacrifice. The shedding of human blood, and the taking of human life on their consecrated altars, was common on Mars in early historic days.

They have a Bible, as we have, a Bible of Old and New Testament Scriptures. While the verbal expressions often differ from ours, yet in substance their Bible is like ours.

The idea that God's displeasure could be

B

2

placated, and his punishments bought off by
blood-sacrifices, remained a prominent feature
in their Jewish church until long after the
coming of Christ. The same idea, in the form
of self-inflicted sufferings as penance, was practised in their so-called Christian churches for
many centuries thereafter.

In one of their libraries I found an interesting old book, published about three thousand
years ago, when their civilization corresponded
with ours at the present time. In this book
I was greatly interested. It treated at length
of their Jewish sacrificial system and its effect
on Christianity. I will quote a few sentences
from it :

"Language is never quite ready adequately
to express new ideas, or, rather, the thoughts
of new systems, either in matters of science or
religion. So at first the new must be expressed
in the language of the old. This fact often
causes too much of the old to be carried over
into the new, and causes more or less ambiguity
and confusion. The old ideas are prone to
stick to the language, even when the language
is used to express the new ideas. Later on,
every science or system gets a nomenclature
and phraseology of its own, when its definitions and lines of distinction can be more
sharply drawn, and there can then be more

accuracy of expression and less liability of misleading or being misled.

"To avoid this danger in the introduction of a new science or a new religion requires a master-mind, one that is master of both thought and expression. Christ had this ability to an unequalled degree. By the use of known experiences, parables, recognized figures, etc., he was able at once in his discourses to distinguish between the new and the old,—between the old objective religion and the new subjective. He at once arraigns not the outward wrongful act alone, but the inward motive,—the state of the heart which leads to the act. And how vividly he draws the line! how clearly he defines the difference! 'Ye have heard that it hath been said, Thou shalt not commit adultery : but I say unto you, That whosoever looketh on a woman to lust after her, hath committed adultery with her already in his heart.' How clearly and vividly this brings the heart-religion into view! Also, 'Ye shall know the tree by its fruit, the fountain by its water, the quality of the heart by the life that flows from it.' But the disciples and apostles were not equally happy in possessing this ability. Christ in his teachings nowhere teaches that blood-sacrifice has any part or place in his religion, but distinctly teaches that the Father will not have sacrifice, other than a contrite heart, a broken spirit.   •

"Yet Christ had scarcely left Mars at the hands of the murderous Jews before the Judaism of the disciples and the paganism of the Gentile Christians began to work up the crucifixion of Christ as a blood-sacrifice, in the offering of which Christ's murderers were dignified as God's officiating priests. This sacrifice was to atone for the sins of all men in all time who accept Christ and believe in him. Such a doctrine finds no foundation in the teachings of Christ, none in the nature of man, and none in the character of God as portrayed by Christ. During the reign of the so-called Christian emperors, when Christianity had been alloyed and begun to deteriorate under state patronage, and the resultant corruption of the priesthood, an attempt was made to lay a basis for this sacrificial theory, by begetting a trinity of persons in the Godhead. So this was also added to the articles of faith, and to call it in question was heresy."

CHAPTER III.

As I have before said, the people of Mars are about three thousand years in advance of where we are, or, at least, their books indicate that three thousand years ago everything relating to humanity coincided with our present condition. By years I mean our years, not theirs. The year on Mars is equal to almost two years on the earth. So, to avoid confusion, we will indicate time there by our own measurements.

Mars, like the earth, has an eastern and a western continent, separated by navigable seas. As here, the eastern was first inhabited. The western was settled by emigration from the eastern. The first settlers went west, either to avoid religious persecution, or with the hope of accumulating wealth more rapidly. Both classes, too, carried with them courage and industry. Both classes exhibited as ruling characteristics personal courage, intensity of thought, strong will, and economy,—just the elements to make a grand population, when so adjusted as to work harmoniously. But the

3*

two classes were not congenial for many years.
One class was in quest of riches, the other of
religious liberty. Their early settlements became colonies of the governments of the Eastern
World, but they were too widely separated from
the parent governments, both by distance and
by sentiment, to render these relations enduring.
So in process of time, after a bloody struggle
lasting several years, these colonies severed
their colonial relations with eastern governments, and, by uniting together, formed a strong
government of their own, wherein the ultimate
political power remained in the people at large.

The Old World prophesied that the new
government was essentially weak in its principles and plan, and would soon go to pieces.
They watched and waited, only to see it constantly growing in strength and in the confidence not of its own people alone, but of the
common people all over the planet. The
thought of self-government was enchanting
to liberty-loving people everywhere,—so they
flocked from the Old World into the New in
vast numbers, and it rapidly became peopled
by all tongues, and all grades of intelligence
and civilization, and all shades of religious
sentiments.

The government being under the control of
the people, it was early recognized that the peo-

ple should be intelligent; so education was popularized, and common schools were everywhere established, and gradually made as free as the air and water to all. In the early history of this educational movement, each nationality desired to have its own language taught in these schools, and, when any considerable number from any one nation were represented in one school, their language was allowed to be taught. But the influence of this was in time discovered to be bad, as it fostered the building up of separate clans of the different nationalities, and stood in the way of that entire unification of the people essential to strength and extended influence. Finally only the language prevailing at the time of establishing this new government was permitted to be taught in the public schools. In this way they became a great people of one language, with their kindred scattered among all nations over all the world.

These western people were filled with enterprise, and, as they increased in wealth, became great travellers. In visiting the homes of their ancestors, in the Old World, speaking only the language of the New World, the ears of the Old World speedily became accustomed to the language of the New. Thus the way was rapidly prepared for the adoption of the lau-

guage of this Western World as the sole language of the whole planet. To prepare it for
being thus adopted, the written language was
improved by making it purely phonetic.

In that age Mars had many large cities.
Idle people seeking employment, and idle people who desired to live without employment,
flocked to these, and everywhere the cities were
the gardens for the cultivaton of vice and crime.
Large wealth was accumulated in the hands of
the few all over the planet, and poverty and
want belonged to the many. The few lived in
luxury, the many in want, and neither class
were serving the high end of their being.
Inequality and unhappiness everywhere prevailed. Severe laws were enacted for the protection of persons and property. Prisons and
almshouses were everywhere and always filled.
Courts of justice were numerous, and were
busily engaged in punishing crimes and settling
property disputes. There was everywhere a
struggle to get property without earning it.
Swindling schemes were constantly being devised, and conspiracies formed to get possession
of property without rendering an equivalent
therefor. If schemers succeeded and gained
riches by their conspiracies, they were lauded
as men of great ability, and immediately took
rank in so-called good society. If they failed

they were outcasts, and punished as criminals. Wealth was the one great desideratum everywhere, all the time; and all else—honor, honesty, justice, friendship, and even religion—was sacrificed on the altar of Mammon. Social position depended on wealth. Coarse, uncultured vulgarity, if backed by large possessions, was received and welcomed into the, so-called, best society; while refined, educated culture, if poor, was excluded. This made the struggle so intense as to foster and half approve the great volume of crime which then existed. The rich struggled to get richer, and this struggle made the poor poorer. The rich vied with each other in luxurious equipages, dress, and living. The extravagant luxury of the rich was a constant temptation to those having smaller yet comfortable incomes to live beyond their means, and often to be guilty of peculations, breaches of trust, and forgeries. In this way vast numbers of young men of great promise were ruined.

For many years after the independence of the Western World, individuals erected small manufacturing establishments wherever they could find cheap power and sufficient population, but before the new government was a century old manufacturing concentrated in cities, and small capitalists combined together

c

and organized on the general plan of our corporations, and erected immense establishments, employing vast numbers of workmen. This tended to the rapid growth of such cities, and the employees of these large establishments were crowded together, having inadequate accommodations, and sacrificing the health, comfort, and often the virtue of their families in consequence. New impetus was thus given to vice and crime.

As soon as such large numbers of laborers were thrown so closely together, they began to organize for mutual improvement. This led in process of time, as employers became more avaricious, to organizations having for their object the resistance of real and imaginary encroachments upon their rights by their employers. These organizations accomplished much good and much harm to hand-laborers. Good, by showing to their employers that they had rights that must be respected. Harm, (1) by tending to establish in their minds the idea that manual laborers were a caste, into which one was born, and the boundaries of which few could ever hope to pass; (2) by severing the cords of sympathy between the laborers and their employers, thereby rendering it more difficult to take an employee into the proprietorship and have him become a co-employer; (3) by establishing uniform prices for labor,—thus taxing the man whose diligence, intelligence, and skill made his services worth much more than the average, to support the one whose ignorance, indolence, and awkwardness made his services worth much less than the average, thereby handicapping diligent skill to reward indolent awkwardness, and lessening the motive to attain excellence in one's calling ; (4) but the worst effect of these associations, and the one which at one time seems to have threatened to turn the wheels of progress backward, was their tendency to destroy that independence of their members so necessary in a government by the people. There was nothing that so rapidly developed the self-governing principles in these Western people as did the free conflict of mind with mind in their direct intercourse in business transactions. Even if a man had nothing to sell but his labor, he was made a stronger and more self-reliant man by himself looking up and bargaining with the man who would pay the most for it ; but in these associations, at one time, they had executive committees, who relieved the individual members from this duty, and determined for them when they should or should not work, and settled the price to be paid for their labor. Under such management the manual laborers became more and more dependent, and were rapidly losing the spirit of

self-control and self-reliance that made them
good citizens of a free government. These
associations about the end of the nineteenth
century had forced nearly the entire laboring
population to join them. This they did by
combining against non-association labor, and
applying disgraceful names and obnoxious
epithets, and often by cruel personal abuse.
Leaders of the associations would harangue
the members with demagogical efforts bitterly
to prejudice their minds against all who possessed property, and thereby aided in building
up a communistic spirit in the land, which
largely destroyed respect for property rights.
The result was a society filled with thieves,
pickpockets, burglars, highway-robbers, and
even with anarchists who would destroy all
government, legislative laws, and society regulations.

Destructive associations were not confined to
manual-laboring classes, but men of property,
capitalists, also combined in large corporations
for manufacturing and transportation purposes.
These associations would devise new means to
oppress manual laborers, by lessening wages
and extending the hours of labor, often dis-
regarding the need of a day of rest, and compelling their employees to labor the whole
seven days of the week. These corporations

would compete with each other in the reduction of the price of their wares, in order to command the trade. This was often carried to such an extent as to result in over-production, and the consequent reduction of prices to such a point that it was impossible to pay the laborers sufficient wages for the adequate support of themselves and their families. Finally these large corporations, to prevent destructive competition, combined in immensely larger corporations, resembling our pools and trusts. These trusts operated by curtailing production, often entirely closing the works of a large corporation, and throwing out of employment vast numbers of people. They took good care to protect their own profits, but showed no regard for the laborers. Prices of products would be increased, but the discharged manual laborers were left without means to buy. In this way the breach between labor and capital grew wider and wider, while the real interest of all demanded that no breach should exist.

Capital did other great wrongs. It bought itself into office, throttled the will of the people, bribed legislatures, corrupted judges, and was guilty of many other evils, which could only be brought about by the wrongful use of money.

Another source of hinderance to a rapid

advance of civilization in the Western World
was found in the condition of what was termed
" domestic service." The scramble for position
in the so-called highest social circles, and the
effort to keep such circles exclusive, had bred
in people of wealth more or less contempt for
labor or laborers. The nearer the laborer was
brought to the employer, the more intense the
contempt seemed to be. The women of wealthy
families disdained manual labor more than did
the men. The result was that women of character were driven out of domestic service, and
took places as clerks in offices and shops, where
they were exposed to greater temptations, and
driven to less healthful but more respectable
service. Their places in domestic service were
largely filled by a lower class, often unchaste
and in many ways dishonest. The children in
these families were necessarily brought in contact with these defiled women, and their minds
were debauched and made familiar with the
worst forms of vice, often before they were old
enough to know the meaning of what they saw
or heard. Such were the homes of many professing Christian families. The heads of these
families contributed large sums to send Christian teachers to foreign heathen, while employing the worst kind of heathen teachers for their
own children, in the back part of their own

dwellings. These domestics were rarely invited to attend church or join in family worship with their employers, and, if invited, were not expected to accept the invitation.

The effect of all these things, and of what grew out of them, on the Christian civilization of the planet, especially on the people of the free Western World, is represented as fearful, and as threatening to turn society back to original barbarism. The nineteenth century closed, leaving everything out of joint and apparently tending to chaos. Even the Christian church seemed almost to have entirely lost its function of character-building. The largest branch of this church would condone all sins except refusal to obey the mandates of the priesthood, and in almost all the other branches heresy, or disbelief in their particular tenets, was the greatest offence, and exposed one to their bitterest anathemas.

The world was filled with great activity and enterprise, but very largely it was the enterprise of greed,—greed for riches or for personal aggrandizement. These riches were generally sought by preying upon each other, rather than by efforts to seize the laws of nature and organize them for the advantage of mankind, in converting idle and raw material to beneficent use.

The only hopeful outlook at that time was the growing spirit of investigation, of broader and more accurate thought. The general diffusion of education and the growth of intelligence were rapidly making men more scientific, logical, and philosophical. People were beginning to recognize the fact that society was disjointed and working at cross-purposes, and many were looking for the destructive element, with the view of extirpating it. Many theories for so doing were being advanced, and many books on this subject were published about the close of the nineteenth and beginning of the twentieth centuries. Some of the theories were plausible, but would not bear the test of close analysis; many were entirely utopian; others had elements of good, but lacked the support of sound foundations. Many of these theories were interesting and made charming reading, but we have neither time nor space for them here. This spirit of inquiry extended well into the twentieth century, and deepened and broadened as it extended. All of the wiser and more thoughtful of these writers early discovered and agreed that the sense of justice, the sense of what was right and wrong between man and man, whether or not it had ever been any stronger, had been debauched for so many generations past that it had become too feeble generally to assert itself in human transactions; hence the almost universal scramble to over-reach and out-wit one another. These writers recognized that any plan or system of reformation, that failed to elevate or restore the sense of justice to its proper controlling influence in the dealings between man and man, must prove a failure. They also recognized the fact that this sense could only be reached by a quickened conscience, and that the conscience of the masses was most effectually reached through the church, —that conscience was so closely allied to the religious sense as to be quickest and most effectually reached through that sense.

It was decided, therefore, by the most advanced and able thinkers that the reform must be reached through the Christian church. But to fit it for this reform work the church itself must be reformed. The Christian church seemed to have strayed far from Christ's teachings. Christ brought his gospel to the poor. When their forerunner of Christ, their St. John, sent his followers to Christ to inquire of him whether he was the real Christ, or whether they should look for another, Christ answered by calling attention to his works, and said, "Go tell John," and, after enumerating several things, added as a climax, "and the poor have the gospel preached unto them." At the beginning

4*

of the twentieth century, on Mars, the gospel was not being very effectually preached to the poor generally. The churches, especially in the cities, where reform was most needed, preached the gospel to the rich, and only very sparingly to the poor; and with shame it is said that in preaching the gospel to the rich it was largely shorn of its life-giving principles. It was fitted for the palates of the rich, and care was pretty generally taken not to offend those palates by anything distasteful.

Most of the churches were costly edifices, finished in gorgeous style, making large expenditures necessary to support and maintain them, —far beyond the ability of the poor to contribute. The rich parcelled among themselves all the desirable seats. Even where a few corners were reserved for those unable to pay pew-rent, the occupants were constantly made to feel their poverty, when contrasting their accommodations with those of people who were able to pay for their sittings. In short, the poor were generally made to feel they were not wanted, even in the churches. The clergy courted the wealthy and those holding high social positions, and took care not to condemn such wrong-doing as was peculiar to those classes.

The churches generally at that time were wedded to certain creeds, formulated hundreds

of years before, at a time when they were peculiarly exposed to false theories and mistaken
views. Many adhered to doctrines antagonistic
to needed reforms.

Early in the twentieth century many leading
clergymen began to urge upon their brother
ministers the absolute necessity of the churches
making restatements of their doctrines. Pre-
paratory to such restatement, many volumes
were written and published, in which were
critically examined the distinctive doctrines of
Christianity with the desire to get back to them
as a church foundation. The further this extended, the more evident it appeared that true
Christianity was the panacea of all the evils
that afflicted governments and society, as well
as individuals.

During the nineteenth century, especially the
latter half of it, the study of science on Mars
had made wonderful strides, and had opened
up many valuable mines of thought, and, what
was of most value, had developed better methods
of investigation, so that it was far easier to distinguish between the true and the false. Investigators were becoming more honest, and
approached questions without preconceived no-
tions and theories to maintain, or, at least, with
the ability to lay them aside, if they had them,
and look only for truth.

Science had, on Mars, up to near the close of the nineteenth century, been confined exclusively to the material world and to theories relating thereto. Yet many of these well-settled theories ran athwart well-settled religious opinions. For instance, theologians had believed that the planet and substantially all upon it had been created out of nothing by a fiat, in six literal days. But scientists demonstrated by the planet itself that such was not the case, but that many thousand and probably many million years were occupied in the work of creation. Again, they had believed that after the planet was created God made, by fiats, full-grown animals, as we now see them, to inhabit the waters, the air, and the land. Also that man was created, from the dust of the ground, in the same way. Scientists conceded that all were made from the dust of the ground, but not by a fiat in their mature form. They discovered that, early in the work of creation, animal life had been brought into existence in a very low and imperfect form,—imperfect as compared with animal life now, but probably perfectly adapted to the state of creation then existing. The air was then thick with unabsorbed nebulous matter which could not have been breathed by animals of to-day. The waters were in the same condition,—thick and turbid,—so the early stages of vegetable and animal life were adapted to this condition of things. Scientists had also discovered that God had established certain laws of selection and survival, under the regular operation of which he had evolved what we now see, even material man.

There were men on Mars, at the time of which we speak, known as materialists, not very numerous, but very loud and demonstrative. They denied spiritual existence, because, by making a chemical analysis of man, they could find no spirit. They denied the existence of a personal God, and held that with man, as with the lower animals, death ended all.

These men were not scientists, but a sort of science-scavengers, akin to what, in an army, are known as camp-followers, living upon what the soldiers throw away. In the same way, they hung upon the skirts of scientists. Many of them were men of culture, of keen wit, bitter sarcasm, and burning oratory, but never scientific, and rarely logical. They had much of the phraseology and the nomenclature of modern thought, but none of its power or methods of analysis, or its spirit of candor. However, their brilliancy gave them a following. Their methods were purely destructive. They tore down, but never built up. They took away a man's faith, but gave him nothing in return. Their aim seemed to be the utter destruction of the religious sense in man. Of course they did much evil, but, unintentionally, they also did much good. In centuries of benighted ignorance, with a corrupt, sensual priesthood, endowed with great power over the minds and bodies and property of the laity, Christianity had become handicapped with false doctrines and practices, until it seemed to be staggering under a load of falsehood. These errors, like ugly warts on the otherwise beautiful face, seemed to invite the ridicule and sarcasm of these enemies of all religion, and thus the more thoughtful and earnest Christian scholars and ministers had their attention called to these errors, and began to devise ways and means to eradicate them. They soon discovered that these errors, or false doctrines, were breeding much scepticism within the church. The pews were beginning to think, as well as the pulpits. Many would quickly recognize a false doctrine when pointed out to them, who had not been sufficiently trained in logical analysis to enable them to distinguish clearly between the true and the false, and so rejected all,—threw away their Christianity because error had become attached to it,—in pulling up the tares, they destroyed the wheat also.

This state of things greatly alarmed real Christians everywhere, especially the more intelligent. Those having the requisite scholarship commenced a vigorous examination of their creeds, determined to find the errors if they existed and devise means for eradicating them.

When their nineteenth century went out and the twentieth came in, this movement was just getting a strong hold of the Christian mind, and the publications and discussions which emanated from the press in the first half of the twentieth century were interesting beyond my power to describe. It is, of course, impossible for me to reproduce here any considerable portion of those publications; so I must content myself by quoting a part only of such as are said to have been most potent in bringing about the present advanced state of civilization and the religious and social unity that now prevail on Mars.

Since the adoption of a universal language on Mars, all the old books of merit, of all the languages formerly used, have been translated into their present tongue and are accessible to all.

CHAPTER IV.

AT that period of thorough re-examination of their platforms and creeds, the theologians and philosophers of Mars went back to first principles in their investigations. They seem first to have grappled the question, " What is the nature of man, and what are his wants?"

It was exceedingly cheering to notice how honestly they seem to have gone at their work. Approaching from all directions and from all shades of belief and disbelief, they seem to have laid aside all preconceptions, and to have searched diligently for the truth, without apparent care as to whether the truth sustained or contradicted their former ideas. Various were the early opinions expressed in these examinations, but, after several years of earnest and knowledge-seeking discussion, and the publication of many volumes of rich thought, the leading minds both in and out of the church began to converge, and find common ground on which they could stand. They came together in a common finding, best expressed in a somewhat elaborate work, published about the middle of the twentieth century.

I have before said that their language is spelled phonetically, and is much more condensed than ours: their thoughts require fewer words for expression. One can read their books almost as rapidly as he can think. This facilitates holding the attention to the subject-matter and makes the reading an easy task. I made copious extracts in short-hand from these publications, and will translate portions of them into English as well as I can. Their Scriptures differ from ours in many respects, yet I cannot do better than to adopt ours as the translation of corresponding passages in theirs.

The author says: " When treating of the conditions of man in relation to immortality, I propose to accept the Mosaic account of his origin and fall, as the same has been commonly interpreted, because, for all practical purposes, that will serve my purpose as well as any other; but in so doing I do not wish to commit myself for or against that interpretation.

"'In the day that thou eatest thereof thou shalt surely die.' Did this mean that Adam should suffer natural death as the penalty of disobedience? Did it refer to the death of the natural body? Adam did eat of the forbidden fruit, but he lived many years thereafter. His

c   d   5

body was akin to all around him. It was of the earth, earthy; the very construction of his body, wonderful though it was, all prophesied of decay and death. The very permission, 'Of every tree thou mayest freely eat,' etc., was an announcement that the bodies of Adam and Eve were subject to the laws of organic matter, of growth and decay, of wear and tear, —in short, of death.

"God said, 'In the day that thou eatest thereof thou shalt surely die.' The serpent said, 'Ye shall not surely die.' If the death referred to meant the death of the body, the serpent would seem to have spoken the truth, for 'in the day' could not have meant hundreds of years thereafter, for in the natural course of events death would then occur anyhow.

"Adam was endowed with a life in addition to that given to the beasts of the field. After being made, as were the other animals, we are told that God 'breathed into his nostrils the breath of life, and man became a living soul.' This life, so distinctively mentioned and thereby so emphasized, meant something more than natural life, something more than was bestowed on the other animals.

"Modern science has made great progress in discovering the processes of evolution, demonstrating that much of what exists is the result of what is called natural law. Scientists generally, however, substantially confess that they meet with chasms which this natural law cannot leap, and which apparently could have been bridged only by creative power. They discover no law of inorganic matter that could evolve the organic. Dead, earthy matter seems utterly incapable, of itself, of assuming vitality or of evolving it. It is dead, and no law or function of dead matter has been discovered that will empower it to beget or assume life. It may be vitalized, but by nothing within itself. The most that can be said of it in this connection is, it is susceptible of vitalization.

"The most persistent efforts have been made, with every conceivable form of analysis and synthesis, to discover in inorganic matter an ability to evolve the organic, but without avail. The chemist may decompose the apple or the potato and determine, he says, its elements, and may carefully weigh each element and find that the sum of these weights is equal to the weight of the whole, thereby showing, to his satisfaction, that he has lost nothing; yet he is unable to combine these self-same elements in their original form. He failed in his analysis to save the *life* with the other elements.

"Life was a creation. The organic called for the fiat of Creative Power. After this creation the herb is able to overcome the inertia of dead matter and set its particles in motion, and lifts them up in opposition to gravitation, and causes them to assume new forms, enter into new relations, and perform new functions.

"Another chasm, perhaps not so broad, lay between the animal and vegetable worlds; but between the animal and the spiritual lay an abyss broader and deeper than that between the organic and the inorganic,—a chasm that nothing below the spiritual could bridge.

"As the vegetable life must reach down into the mineral world and lift up its dead particles and endow them with new functions, and as animal life must reach down into the vegetable kingdom and lift up its elements into new and higher forms and offices: so the spiritual life must reach down and seize upon the animal and endow it with new and loftier powers.

"When man became 'a living soul,' the chasm between the animal and the spiritual world was bridged. Man walked the planet as other animals did, and in addition he trod the spiritual world. He had two lives,—the animal and the spiritual. Through the animal he was akin to all below him, and through the spiritual, to all above him.

"The loss of life is death. Scientists define life to be 'the continuous adjustment of internal force to external relations.' This means, in part, that no finite thing, whether vegetable or animal or spiritual, can live within itself. To live, 'it must keep its internal organs and functions adjusted to the appropriate outside counterpart of its existence, that the one may draw its necessary support from the other.'

"Death, then, would be the severance of these relations, or, in other words, a failure continuously to keep properly adjusted the relations of the internal to the external.

"By analogy we may reasonably infer that exactly the same is true of spiritual life. When man partook of the forbidden fruit, when he sinned, he did nothing to disturb the continuity of the internal to the external bodily relations; hence his bodily life was not lost. There was nothing to cause bodily death, but he did at once, instantly, sever the adjustment of the internal to the external spiritual relations. He cut himself off from his source of spiritual nourishment, and, as a natural, necessary result, he became spiritually dead.

"'To sustain his natural life, man must maintain a continuous adjustment of his internal organs to their external source of supply, such as the stomach to food, the skin to proper temperature, the lungs to air, etc. If the continuous adjustment of the lungs to the air be de-

5*

stroyed, death is the immediate result, or, in the language of modern science, 'Man lives while his bodily organs are in correspondence with their environment, and dies when that correspondence is broken,'—or, in plain, old-fashioned language, he dies when the support of life is cut off, whether from the lack of the external supply, or the inability of the internal organs to appropriate such supply. If he cuts off this supply by his own act, he is guilty of suicide.

"When God said, 'In the day that thou eatest thereof thou shalt surely die,' he did not thereby proclaim an arbitrary penalty for sin, in the sense in which penalties are inflicted by outside authority for commission of crime, but he simply informed Adam of the necessary, natural law of cause and effect, and gave warning that such act would be spiritual suicide. When man deliberately disobeyed God, his spiritual death was just as inevitable, and just as natural, as would be the death of the body when a man hangs himself and thereby shuts the air from his lungs.

"The continuity of the internal to the external relations, or the correspondence of the internal organs to their external environment, being once broken, can be re-established only by creative power. With this view of man,

how vivid and full of meaning are the words
of Christ in his illustrative figure, 'I am the
vine, and ye are the branches ; if a man abide
not in me, he is cast forth as a branch and is
withered (dies), and men gather them and cast
them into the fire and they are burned.'

"If the spiritual life is the only source and
promise of immortality, then, if man died
spiritually, why did he not become as he would
have been if God had not 'breathed into his
nostrils the breath of life'? Such death must
have reduced him to a mere intellectual animal,
—spiritually extinct,—leaving no call or use
for an eternal hell, no necessity for an infinite
sacrifice, no place in the universe for an orthodox
atonement or an orthodox trinity. There would
seem to be no more necessity that the Son of
God should submit to become the victim of the
heathenish idea of a blood-sacrifice for man
than for the ox or the ass or the monkey.

"Man, as a mere intellectual animal, is capable of wonderful culture and development, and
also of a high degree of morality. As a mere intellectual animal he may seek his own interests
in the interests of others. He may conclude
that to be strictly just and honest and honorable
in his intercourse with others will best conduce
to his own interests. He may, for the same
reason, adopt the *Golden Rule* as the rule of

his life, and yet have no spirituality and no part or lot in the future state. This alone is not spiritual life, and is no certain evidence of such life. Mere animal selfishness may lead an intelligent man to do justice and equity.

"The mere universal dream of immortality, the mere universal desire for it, the longing hope for it, are no proofs that the one who dreams and desires and hopes is immortal. So far as this state of mind indicates anything, it tends in the direction of proof that there is something above and beyond our present state, a spiritual kingdom, a source of spiritual life and light, and, perhaps, of the possibility of man becoming fitted to be a recipient of that light and life.

"The worshipping instinct that has seemed to pervade all tribes and nations in all ages of the world is of the same character,—a sort of half-recognized prophecy of man's adaptation to become more than an animal: it is a God-implanted yearning, designed to make man search for the source of the spiritual, and, if possible, to find the strait and narrow way, —the single door through which he may enter its portals and become its recipient.

"We may safely go a little further, and infer that, in his natural state, man may have an inborn spiritual ovule or seed, which, if impreg-

nated,—fructified by the spirit of God,—may
become a 'living soul,'—'a second birth.' With
this view, the 'second birth' ceases to be a figure
of speech, and becomes a literal fact, a real birth,
the begetting of a new existence. If this ovule
is neglected, if God is shut away from it, it
ultimately dries up, dies, and becomes as if it
had never been. If the germ dies, there is
nothing to develop into a living soul,—no
second birth can take place,—'the day of grace
is sinned away.' For this idea we have no
direct 'thus saith the Lord,' yet it makes many
dark places luminous. The 'unpardonable sin'
is then explained on a rational basis. When
a man is once 'born again,'—this ovule once
vitalized,—and afterwards dies spiritually, there
can be no further hope; for, having but one
spiritual germ, and that being lost, all hope
dies with it. So if a man, once spiritualized,
deliberately sins so as to sever his spiritual relations with the sustaining spirit of the Father,
he has committed spiritual suicide.

" The Old Testatment Scriptures are not very
clear in their direct teachings of immortality,
but they clearly teach the mortality of the
finally impenitent. The New Testament, however, is full and rich in its teachings on both
these points. A hereafter is distinctly and

positively announced over and over again;
also, the doctrine that man, on specified conditions, may continue to live in that hereafter;
yet a most careful and critical examination
will find little, if anything, in the New Testament to sustain the doctrine that natural man
is immortal. There are a few passages which,
taken from the contexts, and unexplained,
might seem to indicate a continued existence
of the wicked beyond the grave.

"On the other hand, science, reason, the general tone of the Sacred Scriptures, what we
know of God as revealed to us in the Bible,
in nature, in his providence, and in the person
of Jesus Christ, accord far better with the doctrine that man, in his natural state, is mortal,
and devoid of that kind of life which is lighted
not to be extinguished.

"The Scriptures speak of natural man as
'dead' in his relation to the spiritual kingdom.
'To be carnally minded is death,' 'She that
liveth in pleasure is dead while she liveth,' 'To
you hath he given life, which were dead in trespasses and sins,' 'He that hath not the Son
hath not life,' or is dead. 'Good Master, what
shall I do to inherit eternal life?'—recognizing
the fact that he is without such life. 'They
have eyes, but they see not, ears have they, but
they hear not.' They have no spiritual eyes or

ears, because they are spiritually dead. 'The natural man receiveth not the things of the spirit of God, for they are foolishness to him, neither can he know them, because they are spiritually discerned.' This extract is full of meaning. It not only announces a fact, but gives a philosophical, scientific reason for the fact. One would as soon expect a dumb brute to comprehend a proposition in geometry as for natural man to comprehend what can only be spiritually discerned. He is devoid of the organ that corresponds to the external spiritual relation. He has no spiritual organ in correspondence with a spiritual environment. To promulgate spiritual truths to such a person is simply casting pearls before swine. 'Every tree that bringeth not forth good fruit is hewn down and cast into the fire.' Fire is the most destructive agent in nature. It reduces to its ultimate elements what it acts upon. The destruction by fire is a final destruction ; hence it is so often referred to as the figurative agent in the destruction of the wicked,—an utter destruction. 'Sin reigned unto death,' 'Death reigned from Adam unto Moses, even over them that had not sinned after the similitude of Adam's transgression,' 'The wages of sin is death,' 'The motions of sin did work in our members to bring forth fruit unto death,' 'Sin revived and I died,' 'Sin slew me,' 'Sin, when finished, bringeth forth death,' 'There is a sin unto death.' Many other quotations from the New Testament might be cited to the same effect.

"The Old Testament is full of the same teaching. 'The soul that sinneth, it shall die,' 'The wicked are overwhelmed, and they are not,' 'The name of the wicked shall rot,' 'Thou hast destroyed the wicked, thou hast put out their name forever,' 'Yet a little while, and the wicked shall not be.'

"It is not necessary to extend these quotations further. Whoever will critically read the Bible from the beginning to the end, searching this doctrine, will wonder how he ever believed that the wicked have an eternal existence.

"It is unaccountable, that the prevailing doctrine in the church should so long have been that 'death,' in all these quotations, does not mean death at all, but a miserable, suffering immortality. Destruction, we have believed, did not mean being destroyed, but that everlasting death meant everlasting miserable life. 'Where the fire is not quenched' we have believed meant an everlasting roasting of conscious beings.

"It is much more rational to be more literal in translations. 'Everlasting destruction' means a destruction that has no end, an everlasting separating of the elements, with no chance of recomposition, no resurrection. 'The fire is not quenched' in the sense that it forever keeps the destruction complete. 'Where the worm dieth not' has exactly the same meaning. After devouring the wicked, the worm never dies, but stands vigil forever, to see that there shall be no resuscitation, no resurrection."

CHAPTER V.

THE author from whom I have quoted so largely, and will continue to quote, was educated in the church which corresponds to what are here called the orthodox churches, and, it seems, was a regular church attendant. He evidently was a devout Christian man, and by persistent and honest investigation seems to have worked himself to near the lead of the reform thought of his age. His writings, evidently, had a profound influence in producing the enviable state of society now existing in Mars.

After making further quotations from both the Old and New Testaments in support of the doctrine that death ends all with the unrepentant wicked, he proceeds : " The acceptance of the doctrine that there is no hereafter for the finally impenitent and wicked—no hereafter for any except the subjects of the ' new birth,'— those who are begotten of the Father unto a new life—was, with me, the key that unlocked the kingdom. It is the broom that has swept from the theological heavens the cobwebs and

fogs and mysteries which were the *débris* of
centuries of a Christless priesthood and enthu-
siastic superstition. It brought broad, open
daylight where before was darkness with only an
occasional glimmer or flash of light, just enough
to convince inquirers that there was light some-
where, and to encourage them to persevere and
search for it.

"This doctrine alone relieves Christianity of
very much of that which is odious and unchris-
tian. It relieves God of the blasphemous
charges which his own professed ministers have
heaped upon him. There can be no eternal
hell of torments, no sacrifice of the Son to
appease the offended wrath of the Father. It
at once makes the Father as lovable as the Son,
—infinitely lovable. It takes away many of
the stumbling-blocks which have needlessly and
wickedly been thrown in the pathway of the
earnest seeker after the truth both in and out
of the church; it has removed one of the prin-
cipal sources of infidelity.

"Punishment, with a view to reform, is consistent with goodness. Retributive punishment
may be *just*, in the sense that it is deserved or
merited, but can hardly be denominated *good*.
Eternal punishment must be simply vindictive,
and cannot be reconciled with infinite goodness.
'An eye for an eye,' 'a tooth for a tooth,' 'a

blow for a blow,' were condemned by Christ; yet the church idea of hell ascribes to God himself the disposition to return incomputable billions of blows for one. Thousands upon thousands are driven to the denial of Christianity, simply because they have been led to believe that this hellish doctrine is a necessary element of Christian faith. The attempt of some to obviate the hardness of this doctrine by making the Atonement save all, without regard to character, is repulsive, for the reason that it offers no reward for virtue, but destroys the very foundation of religion, by putting the highest virtue on the same footing with the lowest vice. The theological twaddle about a new trial in the next world is too insipid to entitle it to thoughtful consideration, as it has neither common sense nor Scripture behind it.

"Some may say that the doctrine that death ends all with the wicked is annihilation, and that annihilation is more cruel than an eternal hell of torments. Not so. There is no cruelty in annihilation. It causes no suffering except in anticipation, and this anticipation is a mercy if it leads to an earnest search for the new life. It is no more annihilation than is suffered by all other animals. Death is often a mercy to relieve from pain, and trouble, and decrepitude. The choice of life is open to all, and, if final and absolute death is a terror, it should induce the choice of life. 'The survival of the fittest' seems to be God's law in creation, and is applicable in distinguishing between those who have been born of the spirit and those who have not.

"Seekers after truth have heretofore been told that, to be intelligent Christians, they must believe,—

"1st. That God the Father is omnipotent and omnipresent,—sees all things, knows all things, and is the source of all power.

"2d. That God the Father will forgive no one, however penitent, until the penalty of his sins has been fully suffered.

"3d. That God the Father will accept the suffering of such penalty at the hands of one who never sinned.

"4th. That God the Father will punish with the pains of eternal torments every man and woman (and why not child?) who does not voluntarily accept this innocent sufferer as having suffered for him or her, vicariously.

"Any who will intelligently study these last three propositions, and get their real meaning, will agree in defying any man, however learned he may be, to define the orthodox 'devil' in terms more odious and fiendish than these propositions make God the Father. Their bare statement were almost blasphemy; yet they have long been taught from the Christian pulpit. Strange it is that there are not a thousand scoffing infidels where there is one. But we are told that the Godhead is an impenetrable mystery in our present state, that the relations of the Father and the Son to mankind are sufficiently revealed for the purposes of salvation, and that we have no right to ask more. This might be satisfactory if the church had not portrayed God the Father as a being so unlike a father,—so cold and merciless, and so mercilessly exacting,—and then bid poor human nature to call him Father, and to make him the object of love and worship,—a Father who forgives nothing, but demands in kind the uttermost farthing of indebtedness.

"How different is the Father revealed to us by Jesus Christ! Christ taught us to pray *directly to the Father:* not through Christ as our intercessor or solicitor, not through the merits of his sinless character, set to our credit, not because of his vicarious sufferings for us, not because he had paid our debt in full; but because God was our Father we were taught to go directly to him, pleading only our own character and penitence for transgressions,—' *Our Father* which art in heaven,' ' forgive us our trespasses *as we forgive those who trespass against us.'* Christ taught us to love our enemies, to bless them that curse us, to do good to them that hate us, to pray for them that despitefully use us and persecute us. Why? 'So that ye may be the children of your Father which is in heaven; for he maketh his sun to rise on the evil and the good, and sendeth rain upon the just and the unjust. Be ye therefore merciful, as your Father in heaven is merciful.' How wonderfully near to us Christ brings the Father! How like a real father he makes him! But the Father of the orthodox creed—how cold, and distant, and merciless, and exacting! He demands the pound of flesh from nearest the vitals of Christ,—an infinite Shylock; he denies the direct access of man to him. In his best estate, in his most penitent and contrite mood, when actuated by his noblest and purest and most loyal impulses and purposes, man is altogether corrupt and unfit to say 'Our Father;' but must plead not his own penitence, not his own pure motives, not his own unselfish loyalty, but the merits of Christ set to his credit, and begs to be saved from the torments of hell, not because he is fit or can be fitted for heaven, not because the Father can forgive, but because Christ went to hell in his place, and suffered the whole penalty, paid the whole debt! Oh, what a God! Oh, what a worship! Whence

came this God? Certainly not from the teachings of Christ. Not a vestige of such a God
can be found in his gospels. Whence this worship? Not in the example, not in the teachings
of Christ: both are directly the reverse.

"Profane history gives the 'whence' of both.
This God and this worship had their origin in
two sources: first, the desire of power by those
who professed to be the vicegerents of Christ
on the planet; and, second, the desire to promise final salvation without demanding purity of
life. In this worship personal character counts
for nothing. 'Before God all alike are impure:' so of what use is purity, if impurity
will furnish more pleasure? For all alike
must at last rely upon the merits of Christ.
Under this religion the old church may sell
indulgences for a consideration, and the new
church may take indulgences without paying
for them.

"Is it strange that under such teachings
there is so little that is distinctive in Christian
character,—that in practical life there is so little
difference between the Christian and the infidel?
Is it strange that you must go to the church
register to distinguish between saints and sin-
ners? Christians may practise some forms and
ceremonies that the worldings do not. They
may go up to the Temple every seventh day,

and go through some heartless ceremonies, and
listen to the learned essays, in which the author
tries to appear as learned as possible and yet
say as little as possible ; but in the real life—
in the state of the heart, from which are the
'issues of life' for the whole seven days of the
week, and for twenty-four hours of each day
—this doctrine of substitution, this putting the
righteousness of Christ for our unrighteousness,
furnishes nothing but excuses and apologies for
every pet sin of our natures.

"The doctrine of imputed merit, substituted
righteousness, is the bane of current Christianity, and does a thousand times more to drag
down Christ and his holy religion than does all
the infidelity in the world. It makes righteousness not a thing of the heart or of the life,
but something to be put on like a garment, a
covering, but not in any sense a part of the
real self or character.

"The poor publican's prayer, which Christ
approved and commended, 'God be merciful
to me a sinner,' is a full, complete, logical, an-
nihilating answer to this church idea of the
Father, of the vicarious atonement, and of
imputed or substituted merit. In this simple
but forcible prayer Christ taught two great lessons, both lying at the very foundation of
human salvation : the one, that God is a merci-

ful being, with an ear quickly responsive to
penitence; and the other, that the penitent
man may go directly to God, with no mediator,
no attorney or solicitor to plead his cause, no
intervening priest or potentate, but directly,
pleading only his own penitence. The orthodox church doctrine practically amounts to
taking the position and teaching that Christ
came, lived, suffered, and died that man might
safely live in selfishness, indulgences, and sin.
In the old church (Romish) which embraces a
large proportion of the professing Christians
of the world, Christianity consists mostly in
loyalty to the church and its functionaries,
and has little to do with purity of life and character. The new church (Protestant) of the
orthodox faith might take the same view, and
still be entirely consistent with its ideas of God
and the functions of Christ.

· "It is not meant to assert, or suggest, that
real, genuine Christians are not found in the
church. There are very many who read and
imbibe the real spirit of the teachings of Christ,
without thinking or caring for the doctrines of
the doctors. They are genuine Christians, in
spite of the creeds. Complaint is made only
of the absurd doctrines with which Christianity is unfairly and wickedly handicapped, and
of the natural effect of these doctrines upon

thoughtful minds,—of their influence to impede the progress of true Christianity in an age like this, when everything must submit to the crucial test of logic and science.

"Of course science cannot develop and promulgate a saving religion, yet it is equally true that religious truth will not and cannot deny the truths of science. What is real science is real truth. What is not real truth is unscientific. Science is just as properly exercised in its legitimate field when used to test the accuracy of alleged facts in theology as in chemistry or geology. In its present state science can do but little in the realm of faith or in the field of religious experience. If the things of the spirit can be only spiritually discerned, then many scientists are shut out from this field of observation. But when we talk of the Trinity, of God the Father practising a ruse before the universe, in putting on a show of being so mercilessly exacting of his creatures, yet himself furnishing a blood-sacrifice to himself that may atone for all the wrong outside of himself, we are using a jargon of words and ideas which, if they mean anything, are in violation of all correct thought and thinking. When we talk of substituting the penal sufferings of the innocent for those deserved by the guilty, we again state an impossibility,—a proposition antagonistic to all forms of logic, common sense, and justice.

"Logically, such a sacrifice and such a substitution could be possible only on the hypothesis that a devil, equal or superior to God in power, has the right by conquest of the possession of the human race, and that his occupation is to torment eternally his possessions. Now, God, being good, filled with love and mercy, enters into negotiations with the devil, resulting finally in a stipulation to turn over the Son of God into the hands of the devil for three days, as a ransom for all such as wish to escape the devil's dominion. Now, if there be such a division of the universe, and if God the Father is God of but one corner of it, then the standard church doctrine relating to the Father and the Son may have a show of harmony with logic and reason. On any other possible hypothesis these doctrines are contradictory in themselves, they fly into the face and eyes of all logic and reason, and are repulsive to our sense of justice and to all the better feelings of our natures.

"Science may not yet be able to explain all that is true in Christianity, but nothing that is true in Christianity will contradict science. The world of science and the world of religion are the same world with God, and what is true

in one cannot be false in the other. In matters
of the spirit science can affirm nothing. It can
only deny, and its denial amounts to but little,
for it cannot prove its negations. It can only
say that science fails to find spirit, and therefore denies spirituality. But such denial is
illogical. Science has really no more logical
basis from which to deny than it has to affirm.
All that it can do logically is to say, ' I do not
know.' Yet science has established methods of
thought and investigation which are very useful
in our studies of spiritual matters, especially in
studying doctrines and creeds. The processes
of logic are the same everywhere, whether in
the spiritual or the material world. So, when
the doctor of divinity begins to reason, he is
bound by the same laws of logic as the pro-
fessor of physics, and is open to the same criti-
cisms when he reaches absurd conclusions.

" It is not meant to affirm that natural man
cannot recognize a God. Even science seeks
and worships a first cause. This is the God of
science. The scientist may call it law, or ruling
principle, or first cause, or whatever name his
fancy may give it; but still it is his God, and
may receive his homage,—a God recognized
by the intellect as a rule of action. But what
a God ! What a worship ! This God is deaf
and blind and frigid, and the worship is mere

soulless, intellectual awe and wonder and admiration.

"But more than this, in natural man there may be a recognition of an intelligent, personal Ruler of the universe, and a more or less conscious feeling of responsibility to that Ruler; and the sense of fear may force him into the forms of worship and many religious observances. He may obtain an intellectual perception of immortality, and entertain a hope that in some way he may attain it. The Jewish worship was and is largely of this kind, and much of modern Christianity must be classed under the same head,—a kind of intellectual religion which fails to embrace the heart and character, and yet practises the forms of religion. Then, again, there is much religion that is neither of the head nor of the heart, but a mere form of worship, practised by parents and continued by children, with no special thought or feeling. In many ways we may recognize the existence of a God, and a Christ, and of personal responsibility, without the remotest taste or touch of spirituality.

"There is a way provided for the particles of dead matter to be infused with life, by being taken up into the vegetable world; but it is a narrow way, and comparatively few particles find it. So there is a way for man to become infused with spiritual life by being taken up into the spiritual world; but 'strait' is the gate and narrow the 'way,' and few there be that find it, while 'wide is the gate and broad is the way that leadeth to destruction, and many there be that go in thereat.' The parallel between dead matter and natural man, however, runs but a short distance. The life must come from the kingdom immediately above in both cases. Dead, inorganic matter has no faculty to hear the invitation to come up higher, and no freedom of choice whether it will accept such invitation; but natural man has both.

"God in his wisdom has made man free, in the sense that man is conscious of a power best expressed in 'I will' and 'I will not;' and he has placed before all men, everywhere, *life* and *death*, and left them free to choose one or the other. Even natural man has a 'law unto himself,' in the light of which he can distinguish between good and bad, between purity and impurity, between selfishness and unselfishness; and, if he makes the best use of even that dim light, and feels contrition when conscious of having done wrong, that contrition is accepted as the equivalent of 'God be merciful to me a sinner,' even if he has never heard of the true God nor of the Christ. When he has thus placed himself in line with God, the spirit of

God will breathe into him the breath of spiritual life, and he will become a living soul. In no other way can the beautiful characters which are sometimes developed among the most benighted heathen be accounted for. Paul recognized this when speaking of those ' without the law.'

" Leading scientists everywhere, after the most exhaustive search, are substantially agreed that there is not an iota of trustworthy proof that life has ever, anywhere, appeared independently of antecedent life. No life, then, is spontaneous; and we may go further, and say that no life can beget other life than that of its own kind. Natural man has only his natural life. So natural man cannot beget spiritual life of himself. ' That which is born of the flesh is flesh, and that which is born of the spirit is spirit.'

" Christ clearly taught that spiritual life came with the new birth : ' Except a man be born again he cannot see the kingdom of God.' Exactly what this ' new birth' is, or what the constitutional or structural change or formation may be, is of course all speculation. The theory already advanced seems most rational, most in accord with known laws of evolution,—viz., that man has, as a part of his natural manhood, a seed or spiritual ovule or a germinal principle which, when impregnated by the Holy Spirit, springs forth into spiritual life, a spiritual being,—a literal begetting, a literal regeneration, a literal birth, a new being comes into existence. This, of course, is only speculation, and as such it is offered. It is pleasing to find a natural law which protrudes, if only a little way, into the spiritual world.

"One thing is certain, this 'new life' is of the spirit, spiritual. It is a restoration to the recipient of what Adam lost when he fell. It is the restoration of the dual life. It brings the impress of God's image, for this new being is God's child, it is an immaculate conception, and has a right, in addressing God, to say 'Our Father.' It has the brand of immortality. 'Blessed be the God and Father of our Lord Jesus Christ, which according to his abundant mercy hath *begotten* us . . . . to an inheritance incorruptible and undefiled and that fadeth not away, reserved in heaven.'

" When a man is 'born again,' he is conscious of a new power at the helm. His aims and purposes are changed. A new direction is taken. A new star has appeared in his heaven, towards which he feels himself being guided. With more or less rapidity, his understanding is enlarged, his reasoning powers brightened and strengthened, his eyes and ears are quickened;

7*

he sees more, he hears more, he feels more, he
understands better, he knows more. His new
life soon begins to assume control of his old
life, and the natural man is gradually being
brought under the control of the spiritual man.
The appetites and passions, one after another,
are bridled and held with taut reins; the disposition is sweetened, hatred and revenge give
place to love and forgiveness, and the desire
that others shall experience the same regenerative influence, or new birth, takes possession of
the heart, and leads to sacrificial devotion to the
redemption of mankind. All this is fruit of
the new birth, and the fruit brought forth is the
only evidence of such birth. This fruit is what
should be sought by examining elders, and not
questions of doctrines, in determining a candidate's fitness for admission to the church. If
the candidate is regularly bearing Christian
fruit, it can come only from a Christian heart;
and, however sound one may be in doctrine, if
fruit cannot be produced as evidence, he has
nothing to recommend him. The person who
has been brought thoroughly under the influence of spiritual life is not only upright,
just, and honest, but much more. The highest
standard of human conduct outside of Christianity is the Golden Rule, 'Whatsoever ye
would that men should do to you, do ye even

so to them.' This is judicially just, but it makes self the standard. Natural man may, undoubtedly, live up to this rule. The same idea is expressed in uglier form by 'Honesty is the best policy.' The standard for spiritual man is the one given by Christ to his disciples,— 'Love ye one another; as I have loved you so love ye one another.' The standard of this love was not self, but 'as I loved you.' He forgot self for others. He became poor that others might become rich. As the mountain permits itself to become impoverished to enrich the valley below, so Christ gave of comfort and rest, of labor and self-denial, of home and kindred, of pleasure and life itself, for those below and about him. His love was a sacrificial love, from the cradle to the grave, from the grave to the resurrection, from the resurrection to the ascension. It was the love that loves to 'Do good and lend, hoping for nothing again.' This love is distinctively Christian. It was revealed to the world by Christ, in his teachings, in his life, in his death. This love must regenerate the world.

"Christ did not announce the Golden Rule as his contribution. In citing it, he says, 'Therefore all things whatsoever ye would that men should do to you, do ye even so to them; for this is the law and the prophets,' and noth-

ing more.   It was Jewish justice.   It was
manly dealing, cold and bloodless rectitude, but
did not necessarily involve any heart.   It did
not necessarily mean any more than 'Honesty
is the best policy.'   It was legal justice; simply
'the law and the prophets.'   'The law was
given by Moses, but grace and truth came by
Jesus Christ.'   That broad foundation of love,
a love that reaches beyond self, and home, and
kindred, beyond neighbors and friends, even to
our enemies, to those who hate and despitefully
use us and persecute us, is an untold degree
above and beyond that upon which the Golden
Rule is based.   Christ's life and teachings were
the first announcement to men of such a doctrine; and when, on the cross, he prayed for
his murderers, 'Father forgive them, for they
know not what they do,' he sublimely com-
pleted a revelation never before made to the
world,—a revelation which, if it could become
the basis of society, would right all wrongs,
for it embraces everything that can be efficacious
and redemptive in lifting man from earth to
heaven.   This love comes with the 'new birth,'
—comes with the spiritual,—is born of the
spirit.   This love is the kingdom of heaven,—
the grain which, when sowed in the heart, springs
up into a great tree,—the leaven which, hid-
den in the heart, leavens the whole lump, sends

out its revivifying influence through our whole nature, correcting all that is wrong, sweetening all that is bitter. ' He that soweth the good seed (hideth the leaven) is the Son of man.' Christ first promulgated the doctrine of such love,— redeeming love, cleansing love, purifying love, love that includes enemies, universal love,—a love which, if universally accepted and practised, would abolish all crime and wickedness, all poverty, all sinful love of money, and would convert our planet to a heaven.

"This is not a love to be possessed only by Christ, and by him to be spread over us as a protecting mantle, or shield, to ward off the wrath of God; but a love born in us, planted in the very core of the heart, and thence growing outward and upward and forcing the bad out of our natures, and rendering us fit for the kingdom. This is Christianity. This portrays the great mission of Christ; and how infinitely superior, and more dignified and Godlike, than the religion which apologizes for man's sins, and substitutes the righteousness of another to save him! In God's army every individual stands or falls for himself: no substitutes are accepted.

"This religion, when possessed, easily distinguishes the Christian from the worldling, without examining the church register. The

f

religion of Christ is not a righteousness to be loaned to us, *quantum sufficit*, to balance the account against us ; but a righteousness the seeds of which must be planted in our own hearts, to renovate our own beings, to purify our own lives, and thereby redeem from the thraldom of sin and death our miserable, passion-blind natures, and fit us for the higher, grander, and better lives here, and for the inheritance of a sublime immortality hereafter,—in other words, save us not *in* our sins but *from them.*

"The humility demanded on entering spiritual life is not the humility of self-abnegating servility, it is not a surrender of judgment and reason to the extent of renouncing either the existence or use of these faculties. God nowhere requires this. Christianity addresses itself to these faculties. The humility demanded is only to the extent of making us teachable. It only requires that we take our intellectual faculties with us to the feet of Christ, our great teacher in spiritual things,— take them there free from prejudgment, free from pride of opinion, free from hostility to the truth for which we seek, free as we would take our judgment and reason to an acknowledged authority in science when seeking information concerning material things, thus humbling ourselves in the sense of confessing our ignorance and becoming receptive,—in this respect becoming as little children. All that the teachings of Christ demand is the correct, the best use of our faculties,—the putting and keeping of them in the best possible condition to comprehend and utilize the message he brought.

"It is clearly the policy of God's moral government to respect man's intellect and will in his dealings with man. On no other theory can we understand why he permits man to be sinful, corrupt, and miserable.

"We are told that God made man in his own image,—that is, gave him an independent existence, so far as concerned his power of choice, —created him with a power of will of his own, and a power to use that will as suits him best. He is free to choose life and the things that sustain and develop life, or he may choose death and the things that lead thereto. Why God has thus made man, and thus left him, we may not fully understand. It is perhaps enough for us to know that such is the fact. That such is the fact, universal consciousness most positively testifies. That we are absolutely free to will to do, or not to do, we know absolutely. We may not be always able to do as we will, but we are able to will. As I have said, we may not fully understand why this is so, yet we may see that true happiness is based on true virtue, and that true virtue can exist only with freedom of choice. In a mere machine we cannot predicate virtue. There is in it neither merit nor demerit : it can be neither blameworthy nor praiseworthy. Without free choice man would be the veriest machine,—capable of neither loving nor being loved, honoring nor being honored,—and immortality to such a creature could be neither useful nor desirable.

"Hence, in all of God's dealings with man,—whether in his creation, in the status He has given him, in the manner in which He has addressed him, through the prophets or through Jesus Christ,—He has always and fully respected this independent will-power. He invites, He urges, He reasons, He persuades, He threatens, but He nowhere forces. He everywhere addresses us as rational, independent creatures, capable of reasoning and judging and determining for ourselves, whether we will or will not. The consequence of our choice is placed clearly before us, but we are left freely to choose the good or the bad,—everlasting life or everlasting death.

"Christianity does not profess to convince the self-opinionated, the headstrong, the perverse, the profane, the self-satisfied. It exercises no direct, controlling influence or power over such. When man becomes dissatisfied with his condition and prospects, and inquires for a remedy, then Christianity has for him an important message, and one which, if he carefully listens, he will find is addressed to both his understanding and his heart."

8

CHAPTER VI.

The publication from which I have quoted continues :

"The blessed gospel of Jesus has been nominally preached for more than nineteen hundred years, with a result that must be unsatisfactory to every thoughtful believer. That this gospel contains a panacea for every personal, social, and political evil, few serious and thinking people entertain an honest doubt. It aims to reach every wrong through personal character, to purify the whole by the regeneration of the individuals, to reach the mass through the elements of the mass. The individual is the integer of society, the unit which being multiplied makes society and the state. Society is intelligent, is good or bad, as these integers are intelligent, good or bad. The gospel of Jesus is wonderfully adapted to perfecting these integers, to improving the capacities and characters of these individuals.

"Why is it that this gospel has taken hold of the public mind so slowly? Why have nineteen hundred years of its preaching pro-

duced such meagre results? A large portion
of the population of Mars have never heard
of this gospel. But a fraction of those who
have heard of it have been brought into our
churches. And but a fraction of those brought
into the churches give any evidence of having
been brought under the direct and regenerative
influence of this gospel. Why is this?

" Chemistry is only a little more than a century old, and what strides it has made! The
knowledge of it is eagerly sought all over the
planet, and its books have been translated into
almost every written language by the people
speaking the languages, themselves, without the
aid of missionaries or foreign teachers. All
our advances and discoveries in science are promulgated in all languages, as rapidly as translations can be made. The people everywhere
and always display an eagerness for such knowledge as may be interesting or useful ; yet the
gospel of Jesus, embracing the choicest instruction, and grandly interesting in all its phases,
does not advance except by tremendous push-
ing,—by great human effort and expenditure.
Why this difference? ' Oh,' answers Ortho-
doxy, ' it is because of the natural depravity
of the human heart. The natural heart instinc-
tively and persistently rejects a knowledge of
God and of self, while it eagerly seeks every

other knowledge.' This answer cannot be true, because all science, all knowledge is of God. His word is written in the rocks, the earths, and the waters, in the clouds and the skies, as truly as in the Bible. Some reason other than natural depravity must be found. Have we not diluted this gospel in our teaching? Nay, worse, have we not injected into it that which is unwholesome and distasteful? All people want bread, and seek and accept it gladly. Suppose all bread, before kneading, should be mixed with water in which quassia, or bitter-wood, had been steeped, would it be so eagerly and so universlly sought and used? It prob-ably would not deteriorate the wholesomeness of the bread, yet all the doctors and bakers and millers and grain-raisers on the planet could not make it an acceptable article of food. Now and then one might be induced to take it, with a wry face, as a medicine, but very few would ever choose it for the love of it.

"Now, is it certain that the spirit of evil did not, through the corrupted priesthood in the early ages of the church, inject the extract of a spiritual quassia into our Christianity? Is there not still in our preaching and teaching some of this bitter foreign substance, so distasteful as to cause the whole loaf to be rejected by very many people?"

The author then goes on to illustrate by discussing the doctrine of eternal punishment and the doctrine of substitution, to the same effect as set forth in the last two preceding chapters. He then proceeds to discuss the doctrine of natural depravity, something in this way :

" The church has long taught that, because of a taint received away back, at or near the origin of our race, all men are of necessity born in sin and iniquity, with a natural proclivity to evil, and that all this is because of the fall of our first parents. In other words, that in Adam the whole race fell, seminally, and that, as a consequence, all the following generations were contaminated at the very core of their moral beings. The scriptural foundation for this doctrine is very slight. There is abundant scriptural evidence of the spiritual death of our first parents, and also of the fact that natural man comes into the world spiritually dead. He is born an animal, and only an animal. He is by nature just what Adam was before God breathed into him spiritual life. He is an animal capable of almost unlimited intellectual culture, and is so constituted that God may breathe into him the breath of life, and he become a living soul, as Adam did, and become capable of unlimited spiritual culture. But all this gives no reason why by nature man should be any more set for sin than against it.

"If we will turn our attention to the natural laws of heredity, as discovered and unfolded by scientists, we shall learn all there is of natural depravity, and may learn a valuable lesson as to how we may change its current.

"This doctrine of natural depravity, as preached and taught, is a lion in the way of the radical improvement of our race. It discourages and kills effort at the very point where effort is most effective, and it furnishes an excuse for all the wickedness arising from neglected childhood. It is one of the great obstacles to the complete work of the gospel of Jesus, almost closing the gate to the kingdom. It leaves childhood, the most impressible period of human life, practically, perhaps not theoretically, out of consideration, and waits for what is called the age of intellectual discretion, when the character is already largely formed, and comparatively few can be reached with regenerative influences.

"There are very few scholars to-day, in or out of the pulpit, in or out of the church, who do not accept the general doctrine of evolution as the explanation of God's method of creation. They may differ as to how often it may have been necessary for God to step in and, by his creative energy, bridge chasms which his pre-established laws are supposed to have been unable to leap; and yet that God has evolved the world substantially as it is out of chaotic and sublimated matter, by the regular operation of established laws, nearly all agree. This is now practically demonstrated by science, and is so admitted.

"Again, nearly all agree that the labors and throes of nature, from the beginning, have been its efforts to produce man; that every step of the process, from the formation of the land, the air, and the water, and the first crude forms of vegetable and animal life that inhabited them, was a step towards, a prophecy of, and an element in the creation of man. In other words, man was from the beginning the foreseen end of creation. In making man, God made everything else. Not that God was obliged to 'cut and try,' to experiment, and to throw away failures, until he finally reached man, by a long series of such experiments. God peopled and occupied the planet, in its slow process of formation, with animals and vegetables suited to its condition at the time. God worked then as he does now, by means; God might make full ears of corn, but he does not. He once created a self-perpetuating corn-germ, and allowed that germ to bring forth the full ear, by a proper juxtaposition and co-operation with soil, moisture, heat, air, and light, and the patient waiting for a requisite lapse of time.

"When we say that man was from the beginning the foreseen, the foreordained end of creation, the *ultima thule* of God's creative work, we do not mean man as we now see him, not man as he now is, not man with his strong controlling passions and appetites, not man under control of the brute elements of his nature; but man in his ultimate possibilities, man of whom the best living specimens are only faint and indistinct prophecies. To the production of this man, God has directed his creative energies through the myriads of years past, and it is believed will through long years to come, until this man shall stand forth in his perfection, the fitting climax of creation, the worthy product of the love and wisdom of the infinite God.

"This climax is to be reached not by the creation of a higher genus or species of man, but by an improvement and perfection of the present race. This we argue from the fact that in mankind now there is a longing for, an expectation of, and a deep inner consciousness of an ability to attain a degree of perfection never yet reached. Probably no man lives without a consciousness of ability to be a larger and better man than he now is. This consciousness is not merely a prophecy, but an almost absolute proof that the perfect man is to be found in the highest development of the present race of men. How? When? Where?

"Our civilization, even what we call our Christian civilization, in many cases does not so much expose and remove the elements of barbarism as it hides and covers up. Well-made and well-fitting clothing, and a knowledge of a few conventional rules and cultivated manners, may, and often do, cover up and hide from the casual observer the veriest savage in the world. To others a man may seem refined and cultured, he may sit in church and look demure and solemn, and be prompt and loud in reading his prayers, and yet in heart be a brutish savage. In all his inner sympathies he may yet be on all fours with the prowling wolf and rooting swine, a mere animal filled with brutish lusts and passions.

"Man, having by evolution come up through the brute creation, has legitimately inherited much of the brute nature, and with it the self-indulgence, narrowness, and selfishness befitting such a nature. God has planted the ovule, the germ, of an immortal spirituality, which begets within him a yearning, sometimes very feeble, for purity and uprightness and charity and peace and goodness.

"Thus, man has a twofold nature, each struggling for the supremacy, and each succeeding according to its proportionate strength. If the brute is the stronger, the spiritual is subordinate and made to serve the brute, and in this way man is capable of becoming more brutal than any brute can be. When the divine element in man is mustered into the service of the brute element, man sinks to his lowest depth, and when the brute element is made to serve the divine element, he rises to his highest estate.

"What we call instinct in the lower animals is largely transmitted education, transmitted through so many generations as to have become fixed and typical, and capable of reproducing its kind.

"It has been found in the brute world that an animal's character may be radically changed by a few generations of careful and persistent education and training, so that a new type, producing after its kind, may be developed, and thus the results of the training and education are transmitted to subsequent generations, governed by the well-established laws of heredity. What are known as coach-dogs and the different species of hunting-dogs are all well-known examples of the operation of the laws of heredity. A few generations ago (dog generations) none of the peculiar characteristics presented by these dogs had an existence. It required several such generations of persistent training to establish in them what is now natural and is now called instinct. These dogs will now perform without training the duties which were with laborious patience and difficulty taught their ancestors.

"From these illustrations we may infer two important truths : (1) that much of that which we call instinct and natural tendency is only transmitted education ; (2) that the original nature and character may be radically changed by a few generations of persistent education and training.

"These truths are pretty well understood by teachers of domestic animals, and much practical use is made of them. This transmission by heredity reaches also to dispositions and tempers, to moral character, so far as dumb animals have such character. Hence kindness and gentleness are carefully sought in breeding family horses, cows, etc.

"Is it presumption to assert that the same laws of heredity act with full and equal force in the human family? They seem to be laws of the animal kingdom, and reaching to all parts of it, from the least to the greatest. Every one knows by observation that the pronounced traits of parents are reproduced in their children. Go into any family of several children where the parents are strikingly dissimilar in their ruling characteristics, and we will find some like the father, others like the mother, and some perhaps a cross between the two, and sometimes unhappy because of the possession of conflicting temperaments. Occasionally we will find a child strikingly unlike either father or mother, but, if we trace back the lines of descent a few generations, we are certain to find its prototype.

"Character consists in one's habits of feeling, thinking, and acting. It is formed, or built up, in the formative stage of human life, and that means early life,—infancy, childhood, and youth. This character is a part of the person; we may say it is the person, the individuality, and, when once formed, is almost as fixed and permanent as the color of the eyes. True, it is possible for this character to be changed in after-life, but such change cannot be counted on. 'Can the Ethiopian change his skin, or the leopard his spots? Then may ye also do good that are accustomed to do evil.'

"Even when a change occurs in after-life, it rarely, if ever, reaches the foundation, the base of character, but acts more like the grafted tree, —it improves and sweetens the fruit of the branches, while the sprouts springing from the roots are from the old stock. It is also a curious and instructive fact that the seed-germ of the most luscious apple or peach grown upon a grafted tree produces not after the kind of the graft, but after the kind of the natural tree.

"This brings us to another important, and by far the most important, law of heredity,—viz., it is a law of animal reproduction, as well as vegetable, to breed from primal character, the character established at the threshold of life. Stock-breeders are beginning to understand this law, and are applying it practically. Stock designed for breeding purposes are trained in infancy for the special purpose for which their progeny are expected to be adapted. In a few generations such training always shows marked and satisfactory results. Horses trained to a square trot or a pace or single-foot before they are a year old will transmit the results of such training to their descendants, but such results cannot be expected if the training is deferred until the horse is six or eight years of age. The same is true of any habits formed before maturity.

"The conclusion therefore is that, if children are properly taught and trained and the formation of their habits properly cared for from birth to maturity for a few generations, their natural proclivities may be changed from evil to good. Children are what they are at birth

E g 9

because of the character—primal character—of their immediate or not very remote ancestors.

"In the human family hereditary traits do not reach through as many generations—or, rather, need not—as in the brute families, for two reasons :

"1. Human infancy is more teachable than brute infancy.

"2. Human infancy is much longer than brute infancy.

"The more teachable, and the longer the infancy, the more can be done to change a nature in a single generation. It would take a much less number of generations to change the habits of a dog than of an oyster, simply because a dog has more brains and is more teachable. The human has the longest infancy of any of God's creatures, and is the most teachable, thereby affording facility for a comparatively rapid perfection of mankind.

"If the millennial days, of which we hear much, are ever to come, they must be looked for through the proper utilization of this prolonged human infancy.

"If the time ever comes when 'There shall be none to say, Know ye the Lord, but all shall know him, from the least to the greatest,' it will be after the lessons of heredity are well learned and conscientiously practised.

"Probably more can be done to arrest and change hereditary traits in one human generation than in ten dog generations. Yet, when we see how much has been done by the teaching and training of dogs and other animals,—how by these means new types and new species with new tastes and habits have been created,—is it not astonishing that no systematic, practical method has been blazed out by which children may be so trained and taught as more effectually to eliminate from them the brute element of their natures, or at least to enable them more successfully to subordinate the lower to the higher elements?

"If the passions and the appetites and all the natural inclinations of our children are simply inherited characteristics, transmitted habits of thought, feeling, and action,—as undoubtedly they are,—then, counter or accelerating education having so long to operate upon infancy, the course of the hereditary current may be greatly strengthened if right, or radically changed if wrong, in a single generation, so that the benefit will be reaped in the next generation by a clearer sky at dawn.

"By the term 'education,' in this connection, is meant not merely set lessons, but the whole atmosphere and surroundings of a child that exert any influence whatever upon its nature

and development. All the environments of a
child are more or less educational and go to
make character. His teachers are found not
only in his parents and employed instructors,
but in brothers and sisters and mates, in ser-
vant-girls, nurses, coachmen, and even in the dog
and cat. This education begins during the first
hour of a child's life. At birth a human in-
fant is a mere animal, and the most helpless of
all animal infants. Its first want is food. The
demands of the stomach are the first to have
attention, and indiscretion in supplying these demands often gives a wrong tendency to a whole
life. A calf or a pig is fed as its health or
growth demands, without regard to its crying
for food between times of feeding, and thereby
it soon learns to bide its time in patience, or, in
other words, brings its appetite under control
of the will. But the child is generally caught
up and fed every time it cries or worries, with
no regard to its health or actual want, and
thereby a majority of children are made glut-
tons before they are a month old, or, in other
words, the will is brought under control of the
appetite. Many parents recognize and admit
this in the subsequent government of their
children, and reward good behavior by sweet-
meats, and punish misdemeanors by denying
something the appetite craves; and yet they

will charge to natural depravity a son's glut-
tony or drunkenness, when in fact it is the immediate result of parental training. The boy
who is at the beginning of life taught well the
lessons of self-denial and self-control, so taught
that the lessons become habits, will never be a
glutton or drunkard. If parents would exercise as much judgment and sense in the care of
their children as of their dumb animals, there
would be little occasion to invoke natural depravity as a scape-goat for their own blunderings. Nature does not deprave childhood
a thousandth part as much as bad education
does.

"If these views are correct, what a field is
here opened for parents, and teachers, and
preachers of the gospel! It is the practical
channel, and the only one, open for the redemption of our race. Our Saviour said, 'Suffer
little children to come unto me, and forbid them
not, for of such is the kingdom of heaven.'
That is, the kingdom of heaven is made of
little children,—not children merely, but *little*
children. If we would build up the kingdom
of heaven, little children must constitute our
material, our brick and mortar, for so doing.
Christianity must be worked into character as
its proper foundation, its warp and woof,—not
dogmatic Christianity, but practical Christian-

ity,—truthfulness, honesty, faithfulness, sincerity, self-control, self-denial, perseverance, patience, cheerfulness, sweetness of temper and disposition, sacrificial love, etc. Training in these should begin with the first breath of life, and never be relaxed until thoroughly inwrought into character. Such training reaches to generations unborn, and those who administer it may feel that they are teaching the ages to come.

"A few generations of such training and teaching, and the world will hear no more of natural depravity as a religious dogma.

"When the Christian ministry, the public teachers, the heads and hearts of Christian parents, are made fully to comprehend the power of heredity, and the influence of education and training upon it, then will begin the dawn of the day when 'all shall know the Lord.' Not that children will then come into the world Christians; but they will come with a natural adaptiveness for spirituality, and will take to Christianity as children now do to deviltry, and we may rely upon it, that the spirit will be born into every heart that is prepared for it. God will inhabit every temple fitted for his habitation.

"The idea that reading, writing, and arithmetic constitute education is very properly ridiculed, yet little more is aimed at in any of our systems of education, at home or at school.

"In our higher institutions, our colleges and seminaries, the sciences are added to the rudiments; yet it is on the same line, in the same direction, as reading, writing, and arithmetic,—all looking simply to intellectual attainments.

"Every one is conscious that body and intellect are not the whole of a man,—that there is something more,—and we are also conscious that that 'something more' is of greater importance than body and intellect, and that it is likewise susceptible of education and development. This 'something more' has not had in our educational work sufficient attention even to give it and its elements a nomenclature. Our language is poverty-stricken for words with which to point out the means of educating this third and most important element in man.

"In olden times that portion of our natures not purely animal was divided into *head* and *heart*. Some have divided our immateriality into *mind* and *soul*, but, for many reasons, this is indefinite and unsatisfactory. Others have given us the threefold division of *intellect, sensibilities,* and *will,* but many treat *will* as a function rather than an attribute.

"But, whatever may be the classification, this 'something more' is the divine element in us,—the spirit-germ,—that attribute of the soul which, if properly directed, loves, and from which flow sympathy, generosity, magnanimity, gratitude, forgiveness, charity, and all the good feelings, or, if neglected or misdirected, gives rise to hate, revenge, animosity, cruelty, and all the bad feelings and desires. In short, it is the source of all our thoughts, desires, and actions which have moral character, and is the seat of our emotional nature. It is the attribute of our nature which makes us social beings, and binds us together in families, communities, and states. Yet, of all the faculties, while of infinitely greatest importance, it is most neglected in the training and education of the young.

"This element, like the intellectual, is at first only germinal, and is developed by educational influences. These influences, in general, are such as chance throws around a child, while order and selection are exercised in the development of the intellect. If the intellect was treated as the sensibilities are, children would all be idiots. If no education reaches the intellectual germ, the child grows up an idiot. If no education reached the moral germ, the child would grow up a moral idiot. But, as I have already said, all the environments of a child constitute educational influences. So, with no systematic or designed teaching, these germinal elements, under the stimuli and demands of our animal natures, will grow, and become more or less strong, only in a direction at antipodes with the perfect man,—strong, with the God-element harnessed in the service of the brute-element. The demands of the animal nature are the demands first proclaimed, and they are loudly and persistently proclaimed, and, if thoughtlessly or carelessly indulged, will rapidly grow in number and persistency until they become overpowering.

"The protection of the spirit-germ by merely shutting the child away from bad influences is not good education, and does not necessarily conduce to healthful spiritual development. It may conduce to innocence, but mere innocence is spiritual idiocy. The moral nature of a child can be properly developed only in contact with the world in which it is to live. It must cultivate the power of choice, and form the habit of choosing the right, and, above all, it must cultivate the power and habit of resisting and overcoming the wrong. The perfection of our race can never be reached through the nunnery and monastery.

"Even the intellect, for its best development, must rely largely upon the illuminating and guiding power of this God-element. Our purposes, and the strength and vigor of our purposes, and consequently the power of our wills, are from this element. How many very learned men are mere intellectual drones in society, simply because they lack purpose and will-power.

"Man's character is just what the development and general tendency of his moral nature has made it, yet character-education plays a minor part in all our systems of education.

"This is made conspicuous in the anxiety of almost every mother when her son is away at college. She knows his intellect is being well cared for, and she also knows his heart is being neglected. Character-education is always progressing with every boy and girl, either under intelligent and wise direction, or under the haphazard neglect of chance, and in a majority of cases the students are matriculated in Prof. Chance's classes. Occasionally an instructor is so well informed about these matters, and is so thoroughly imbued with the love of the pure and the good, and so wise in his influence and counsel, as to reach the high level of a genuine character-educator, and every student unconsciously becomes a better man, and leads a better and more successful life, because of having been under his guidance and influence.

"How to accomplish the end here suggested is and should be a great question. In educa-

tion, as in everything else, in a government of
the people, it is very difficult to get much in
advance of the demand. At present the scramble for wealth is so great that all our people
call for is reading, writing, and arithmetic,—
simply the education of the intellect and the
hands. They are afraid of too much integrity
and conscience, as these functions are liable to
awaken too many scruples as to the methods in
business affairs. They would rather trust to
luck for character. Character is of so little account that even many of our nominally Christian parents turn the formative years of their
children over to nurses and servants who are not
capable of teaching even reading, writing, and
arithmetic, and who have no more interest or
care for the character of their charge than if
the children were so many puppies. Character-
education is not appreciated. Its importance is
not valued even by our Christian people, nor by
our Christian pulpit. There is little demand
for it. All reliance is placed on ' *conversion.*'
The children are educated for the devil, and
then their conversion is sought through the
Sabbath-school and the pulpit, forgetting the
inspired interrogatory, ' Can the Ethiopian
change his skin, or the leopard his spots?'
This Scripture interrogatory is brimful of real
life and sound philosophy. It ought to be

burned into the palm of the right hand of every father and mother and teacher and preacher, so as at all times to be before the eyes of every person responsible for the habits, thoughts, and feelings of children.

"Of course God *can* change the skin of the Ethiopian. He *can* change the spots of the leopard. He can make water run up hill. But we cannot reasonably expect him to do either. It would be just as rational in us to erect a water-wheel on top of a hill to drive machinery, and then get upon our knees and devoutly pray that God would make the water run up the hill and over our water-wheel, as to turn our children over to ignorant nurses, corrupt servants, and thoughtless and giddy teachers, and then hope to save them by prayers.

"The voice of pulpit eloquence in thunder tones must ring in Christian ears, on the crime and wickedness of this gross neglect of child-hood. Good people who appreciate this matter must everywhere write and talk and teach until people are awake, and Christians renovate their homes and direct their thoughts and their hearts more to their children. Then we may expect the demand for a higher, deeper, purer education, and none but such as are masters of this truer, better education will find places as instructors in our schools and colleges.

"To teach a child to become master of arithmetic is important and useful, but to teach him to become master of his appetites and passions, to become honest and trustworthy, gentle and generous, forbearing and forgiving, merciful, kind, and just, persevering and zealous, is of infinitely greater importance. If this is done, beginning at the dawn of life, it is done not only for life but for generations yet unborn. When these principles are understood, appreciated, and practised, there will be no doctrine of natural depravity, and man will begin with his face towards the Lord and his heart aglow with love towards all mankind. The animal-element of his nature will be subordinate to the God-element, and he will begin to cut loose from his brute inheritance, and shake off the dust from the ground which now adheres with so much tenacity. Even in this world, man will yet be of heaven, heavenly.

"Does the reader ask when this will be? Who can tell! 'The mills of the gods grind slowly,' but they keep grinding. With evolution a thousand years are but as a day when they are past."

This publication further discusses the doctrine of natural depravity, and supports the view that the ordinary laws of heredity common to all animals, human and brute, account for all the natural depravity found in man, and insists that it results from false training and neglect. Chapters are presented in which these views are reconciled with those passages of Scripture on which theologians relied to sustain the doctrine of natural depravity, as taught in the orthodox churches.

The most evident single cause of the wretched condition of society at the time the works I quote from were written, was the very feeble condition of the sense of justice in mankind. I will quote a few more paragraphs on this matter :

"The sufferings and the alarming discontent pervading society everywhere seem to arise largely from an almost entire absence of the sense of justice in human transactions. Men in dealing with each other rarely ask themselves the question, Is it just? is it equitable? but simply, Is it legal? Can I do it and not render myself amenable to the law? In this way men —even professing Christian men—will falsely represent what they have to sell to obtain more than it is worth, and will depreciate what they wish to buy so as to get it for less than its real value. This they will do to the full extent that the laws will permit. They will take advantage of a man's necessity, compelling him to sell his labor or his goods at less than they are worth, simply because they can do so. The exaggerated value attached to wealth, and the long practice of obtaining it without thought of rendering a full equivalent therefor, have so benumbed and paralyzed the sense of justice that it rarely asserts itself in transactions between men. Those possessing wealth are generally in a position to dictate terms to those without it, and they usually dictate hard terms. This breeds a spirit of discontent with the poor, and threatens the stability of society. It leads to the discussion of remedies, and develops extreme communistic ideas. Many advocate that the state should take possession of all property, thereby reducing all men to the same property level, and then all be evenly compensated for what they do, and thereby break up property distinctions. The advocates of these schemes forget that the whole can be no better than the sum of good found in the individuals. And in estimating the sum we can count only the excess of the good over the bad in the individuals. As men now are, the sum total of the good in business management in society, after the deductions mentioned, would not be a large sum. The fallacy is in supposing that society can be better than the individuals composing it. The fact is, society can be improved only by improving its members. It will be better when the individuals composing it are better, and not until then. A corporation, morally, is an embodiment and agent of the morality of the stockholders and directors. If we would make the corporation just, we must develop the sense of justice in its stockholders and managers. If we would have society and government just, we must develop the sense of justice in the majorities. The stream will not rise higher than its source. The sense of justice must be made strong in early childhood. Children must form the habit early and strongly of being just and equitable in all they do. '*Quid pro quo*' should be their motto reduced to practice. A few generations of such teachings will banish many of the wrongs of society, and fairness and equity will become the rule in the dealings between man and man. Until then society will not stand on a solid foundation. The work of beginning this education must not be delayed, for society cannot long continue in its present discontented and complaining condition."

CHAPTER VII.

THE doctrines quoted in the preceding chapters correctly exhibit the general trend of the intelligent sentiment of the first half of the twentieth century on Mars. About the middle of that century scientists, and more advanced and scholarly theologians of all denominations, were substantially together in their recognition of certain facts,—viz. :

1. That there must be secured some great social changes, or society would lapse into a semi-chaotic state, with an increase in all forms of crime.

2. That the needed social change consisted largely in a demand for the better development of some of the attributes of man's moral nature, which had been so little used as to become enervated, enfeebled, and almost extinct, such as the sense of justice, the sense of right and wrong, the sense of brotherhood of all mankind, etc.

3. That these principles were so nearly allied to the religious sense that their revival and building up must be looked for through the Christian church.

4. That, before the church could be equipped for this great work, itself must be reformed, by removing needless stumbling-blocks that had become incorporated in its creeds, and were being venerated, not for their origin, but for their age.

5. That the churches should, in view of the light kindled by modern thought, revise their creeds and make a restatement of their doctrines.

The united opinions of advanced thinkers had great influence on the general public, and especially upon well-informed and thinking people. The pulpits were gradually opened to the spirit of modern thought, and particularly to that feature of modern thought which was a revival of the direct teachings of Christ. The demand of the more intelligent of the clergy for a restatement of the church doctrines was awakening great interest, and obtaining a quite general assent, even among those incompetent to investigate for themselves.

General assemblies and general conferences of the various denominations were beginning to appoint committees to examine and report the changes that should be made in their creeds. These committees investigated and discussed the subject in all its phases, and, while all seemed to recognize its propriety and the necessity of such a restatement, yet no two committees, and rarely any two individuals of the same committee, could agree upon one creed. This discussion and these efforts continued for several years. New committees were often selected by the various denominations, but with no better success,—they could get no nearer to an agreement. At first it had been hoped that in the readjustments many denominational lines would disappear, but as they progressed there was a danger that not only all the old lines of separation would be continued, but many new ones established. It was often found, when men began to think and investigate, that in the same denomination, and even in the same church, there were often wide divergencies on doctrinal points.

In God's providence the right man always comes forward when needed, and the times are ripe for him. Mars needed a wise, far-seeing man at the time at which we are writing. The church needed more than a prophet. It seemed as if the church was in danger of going to pieces, so rapidly were dissensions and divisions springing up.

The needed one came. He brought out a little volume of less than one hundred pages, the reading of which settled the whole question and brought order out of chaos. It not only prevented further divisions, but also planted the seed that resulted ultimately in blotting out all denominational lines and made the church a unity. I will quote a few pages from it:

"The unhappy condition of the church at this time presents a great lesson for Christian people. We have all had our creeds and codes. Each denomination has had a creed of its own, and the people have gone to this church or that according as the creeds corresponded with what they supposed they believed. Very many believed, not as a result of their own investigation, but because of the beliefs of those with whom they were associated. Our creeds have been our foundations. It was supposed that these creeds clearly expressed the religious faith and opinions of those who subscribed to them. But the events of the last few years demonstrate the contrary. Our creeds have not been our bonds of union. It has been our ignorance of these creeds that has held us together. As soon as it ceased to be heresy to question the truthfulness and propriety of these creeds, and we were invited to turn upon them the broad and penetrating light of the middle of the twentieth century, we find that they cease to be bonds to hold us together, but, on the contrary, are sources of discord and disunion. As soon as these creeds are examined with the view

of restating our doctrines in forms more in
keeping with the general advance of intelligence, we are astonished to find that they express the real belief of no one. When we make
efforts to frame codes of doctrines, we find it
impossible for any denomination to agree on
any creed that will actually express the beliefs
of any two persons, to say nothing of a congre-
gation or a great denomination. The truth is
we have never believed our own creeds. We
have simply accepted them as our bonds of
union, without stopping to think whether they
do or do not express our real sentiments. Many
of us are in this or that church, more on account of social influences than because of any
particular creed. As soon as we turn the light
upon many of these creeds, they dissolve into
thin air; thus our bond of union is gone, and
chaos prevails. Such must, from the very nature of things, be the case. It is difficult to
find two thoughtful investigators who will or
can ever exactly agree on any statement of
beliefs, on any subject, outside of mathematics.
A code of doctrinal beliefs can never be a compromise among honest men. For we must believe, or not believe. It is not in our power to
believe this and disbelieve that to accommodate
a friend, or because he is willing to do a like
thing for us. Consequently no considerable

number will ever agree on one code, unless they
perjure themselves, or shut their eyes and ears
and accept it without examination. For at
least two generations past, the great body of
church-members have subscribed to creeds portions of which they could not believe. Yet,
to become members they were required to affirm
that they did believe. I do not mean to assert
that they affirmed their belief in that which they
disbelieved. It was non-belief rather than
disbelief. At the present time the people in
the pews are becoming too intelligent thus to
accept and commit themselves to anything. So
the day has passed when creeds can be made the
basis of church organization. Such a basis was
applicable only to times when the pulpit monopolized the thinking and dictated doctrines.
Now we must elsewhere seek a basis on which
to organize.

"While no considerable number of intelligent Christian men can agree upon a code of
doctrinal beliefs, yet all will substantially agree
as to what constitutes a Christian character and
life, because in Christ we always have the
model before us.

"Why not, then, drop the whole discussion
of doctrines, and cease to rely upon uniformity
of beliefs as a basis of church union? Why
not make Christian character the test of church

membership? Would not this tend to developing more of heart instead of head religion? If the heart is right and the life flowing therefrom pure and charitable, what matter about the beliefs of the head? If the head be right and accept the whole creed, while the heart, the life, and the personal character are all wrong, why should such become church-members and assume the name of Christian? We can agree on what constitutes Christian life and character, and we cannot hope to agree on anything better. Let Christian character, then, be the standard, the yard-stick by which to measure applicants for church-membership, and we cannot go far astray. Let the violation of such a standard be proper matter for reproof and discipline.

"Such a standard will tend to direct the attention of all more to the heart and life. With such a standard in place of our creeds, we shall hear and see much less of materialism, infidelity, free-thinking, heresy, etc. The line of separation then will be between the pure and the impure, the honest and the dishonest, the just and the unjust, the benevolent and the malevolent, the chaste and the unchaste, the forgiving and the revengeful, the kind and the unkind, the loving and the hating, the charitable and the selfish, the true and the false, the God-like and the brute-like.

"Is not this exactly the line marked out in the teachings of Christ? Can there be any other line of division having Christ for its authority? Would not such a standard induce very large numbers to take sides with the church who are now arrayed against or indifferent towards it?

"Such a standard for church unity would be a broad basis for all individual and social reforms. Injustice would be proper matter for church reproof and discipline. This fact alone would tend to awaken the sense of justice in men, a sense so dormant as to have almost entirely dropped out of business transactions. Such a standard would make the church what it always should have been, a great character-builder. It would make it the great institute of reform; its shoulder would always be at the wheels of civilization, rolling them forward; it would be the evolutionary instrument, in the hands of God, for lifting humanity to its highest altitude, the altitude of the longed-for perfect man.

"Such a church standard would renovate our families and awaken our fathers and mothers to their responsibilities. It would put a new spirit into our public and private schools and all our educational institutions. They would have their attention more earnestly turned to character-education, to true life. With such a standard, God would be found in our school-books and literature and in the curricula of our colleges. The belief in an overruling God would become universal. It probably is nearly or quite so now. Men deny our definitions of God,—they deny the character we assign to God, and make themselves think they do not believe in God ; and we stigmatize them atheists. Our creeds have made infidels. Our creeds have filled society and the church with unbelievers."

The publications of that period show that these suggestions came at just the right time, and were very soon adopted by the various denominations, so that soon after the middle of the twentieth century denominationalism had almost disappeared from the Western World, and in the Eastern World the work was making good progress in the same direction. As denominationalism died out, doctrinal sermons were much less frequent, and brotherly love much more abounded. As character was the test for church-membership, the influence of the church was almost wholly directed towards character-building, and soon became immensely powerful in its ability to correct and direct the lives of men. Christian parents began to recognize the fact that, if they would save their children, they must begin the work of salvation with the beginning of life. The habits of chil-

dren were watched with the greatest solicitude.
To neglect childhood was an offence against
Christianity, and subjected parents to censure
and church discipline; consequently a much
larger proportion of children embraced spiritual
life and became church-members than under the
old creed arrangement. In fact, within two or
three generations after the adoption of the new
plan, almost all the children of Christian
parents became Christian. The missionaries
carried the heathen a new gospel, the real gospel of Christ, as proclaimed by him when in
the flesh,—love to God as Father and love to
man as brother. This gospel was gladly received all over the planet. There was no waste
of either time or money by different denominations contending for precedence in the same
missionary field.

The plea for a Christian character and a pure
life was a plea that met no opposition. It left
room for no infidelity and no heresy. There
was no ground on which to stand to oppose the
work of the church; so Christianity abounded
everywhere. The publications of that period
show that by the close of the twentieth century
the public mind was largely cast in the Christian mould. Men were esteemed and took social
position according to their real worth, regardless
of the amount of their possessions.

To strengthen the motive, to cultivate personal integrity, and to cancel to some extent the great advantage given to wealth, the various governments began to repeal all laws for the collection of debts, so that by the middle of the last half of the twentieth century no such laws were left among their States. This made personal integrity a man's stock in trade. When a man wanted credit, no inquiries were made as to the amount of his wealth. On the other hand, the inquiries were, Is he honest? Is he honorable? Does he do exactly as he agrees? This stimulated parents to a watchful guardianship of the character and habits of their children. It greatly aided the church in its office of character-building. Truthfulness and reliability were placed at a high premium, while, in the same ratio, deception, falsehood, and trickery were rendered more odious and disgraceful. Wealth began rapidly to lose its charm. Its great power was gone. The sense of justice was becoming comparatively strong, and the habit of rendering an equivalent for what one obtained was pervading all departments of society.

The cultivation of habits of temperance, frugality, and industry among the poor and laboring people was rapidly driving poverty from the face of Mars. Labor became respectable, while idleness and indolence, whether in rich or poor, male or female, was rapidly becoming disreputable. The discontent and the danger arising from it, which had formerly so threatened the very existence of society and good government, had nearly disappeared, and almost all were contented and happy. Labor obtained its equitable share of profits, and thereby friendly relations were established between labor and capital. Capitalists and laborers discovered that their necessary relations to each other were such that mutual good feeling between them was essential to the success and happiness of either. Neither could suffer without the suffering being shared by both. As soon as capital became unjust, labor became disloyal, and disloyal labor could never profit the employer. It was only when each worked for the interest of the other that both flourished.

As money began to lose its power to secure social position to its possessor, it began to lose its hold upon the hearts of men. When integrity and intelligence gave better position and more power to their possessor than money did, money shrank in value in the eyes of men, and integrity and intelligence became of greatly increased importance. Wealth was not within the reach of all, so while wealth was the desideratum of life many were of necessity poor; but integrity and intelligence were within the grasp of all. They differed from wealth, also, in that they could not be monopolized. However much of them any one took, the supply was not diminished, and all might drink long and deep at their wells.

The schools rapidly took high ground as character-educators. They recognized the wide difference between building and growing. Building is adding to the outside, while growth is from within. The old method of making character was the building process. The outside was somewhat reshaped; it was smoothed off and polished, so as to look pleasing to the world. It was filled up a little here, and rasped down a little there, so as to conform to the conventionalities of society, but all inside the surface was neglected. Sometimes this neglect was from gross indifference, sometimes because of ignorance, and often because of the prevalent doctrine of natural depravity, which led even good people to the conclusion that nothing radical could be accomplished in the way of improving a child's character until it reached years of discretion, when "conversion" might be hoped for.

But when the laws of heredity came to be understood, the old doctrine of natural depravity gave way to a more reasonable explanation of the evil tendencies of children, and then a

11*

more rational method of training childhood commenced. Instead of merely polishing the exterior, to conform to the demands of polished society, the new method sought to develop the right kind of feelings and motives and sentiments and dispositions, leaving the outside to conform itself to these qualities. This was making character by growth, and, after a few generations of training, it became a natural growth. The bad tendencies were suppressed at the beginning and not allowed to become controlling. The absence of foolish indulgence, the absence of all stimulants in both food and drink, and the entire discontinuance of the once prevalent habit of controlling children through the appetites by denying what the appetite craved as punishment, and satisfying its craving as reward, and the early development of self-control and self-denial in children, had after a few generations produced almost a different race of beings.

Before the close of the twenty-first century, crime had almost disappeared. Intoxicating liquors were no longer made or sold, as there was no demand for them. Education by parents and teachers and preachers had fully done what the philanthropists of many generations had failed to accomplish by legislation and courts. The courts had but little to do, and

every year their work was becoming less and less.
Legislative bodies also did much less. It had
been well learned that reforms could not be successfully worked through legislation. The time
had been when any one who got in mind some
great good that society needed would appeal to
the legislature and secure the enactment of a
law to enforce his ideas upon others. The
most of these laws then became dead letters
upon their statute-books, because of the indis-
position or unwillingness of the people to enforce
them. Often these reforms were desirable, but
the reformers began at the wrong place. They
attempted to build what could be secured only
by growth. They had not been students of
evolution. They had failed to discover that
God's law of evolution was development, that
it worked from within outward. It is true,
however, that outside influences, surrounding
circumstances, environment, had much to do
in evolving the desirable and suppressing the
undesirable. They finally learned that the
survival of the fittest was as applicable to the
dispositions and appetites and other traits of
character as it was elsewhere in God's providence.

It was only when mankind had discovered
and recognized these laws that the progress of
true reforms was anything commensurate with

the efforts expended. It was only when it was discovered and understood that society as a whole can never be much better than the average of the individuals of which it is composed that attention was sharply turned to individuals. All proper effort in this direction was followed by good effects, and finally culminated in better and more lasting results than had ever been expected or hoped for by legislation and judicature.

When in the work of creation God reached man and gave him a free will, a power of free choice, and an intellect capable of unlimited cultivation, he left him with such equipments to evolve the perfection of his race, to work out his own salvation in the light of such revelations as he might make.

It was evidently not a part of God's plan to reveal in tangible form to mankind what man in his natural state is capable of finding out by the proper development and exercise of his own faculties. God might have revealed to us the constituent elements of matter, all the formulas of chemistry, and thereby have put physical nature far more completely at the service of man, and thus added greatly to human support, ease, comfort, and luxury. He might have revealed all the laws and combinations of mechanics, and thus have put it within the ability of all men to relieve themselves from excessive toil and drudgery. He might have revealed to us the constitution and elements of our own bodies, their functions, and the exact laws of health and physical life, the causes of disease, and the true remedy for each and every physical ailment. He might have revealed to us the best form of civil government, the true science of sociology, and thus have freed the world from poverty and tyranny and all the distress arising out of bad government. A thousand other things about which man now knows but very little or nothing might have been brought to light, and made subservient to the use of mankind, by a direct revelation from him who knows all things. But, as before stated, it seems not to have been a part of God's plan to reveal directly to man what he can learn by the proper exercise of his natural faculties when developed as they may be. In his wisdom God left labor, and want, and distress, and starvation, and pestilence, and inequality, and tumult, and wars, and usurpations, and tyranny, and the thousand other ills to which human nature was exposed, to goad us on in our efforts to learn what good things God has placed in the natural world, and within reach of our natural faculties. He has established in the natural world a system of natural

i

laws, within the reach and scope of the natural intellect, and, by a compensatory system of natural rewards and punishments, has placed before man to entice him, and behind to goad him, every inducement to study and learn. This studying and learning constitute the natural food for the intellectual growth and development of the race. To give all this by direct revelation from the source of all knowledge would take away the very ailment on which intellect grows, and would leave mankind a race of pygmies, unable to understand or appreciate a revelation, while God would have them intellectual and moral giants. We may reasonably conclude, therefore, that God has not revealed and will not reveal in language or life what man can find out by the proper exercise of his natural faculties. We need not, therefore, look in the Divine revelation nor in the life of Christ for the solution of questions of science or of sociology, nor for systems of government, whether of church or state, nor for organizations for charity or for commercial intercourse and relations; for all these things are within the reach of the human intellect when properly applied and directed.

But the province of the natural intellect, as now evolved, is bounded by the natural world. The natural intellect has no eye to see beyond the natural world, and no ear to hear from beyond. It may have a dreamy longing for something, but it sees it not, it hears it not, it feels it not, and it knows it not. It may analyze and decompose and study elements. With the microscope it may go down among the ultimate atoms, but it finds no beyond there. It may study the planets and stars, and with the telescope may peer into the immensity of space and discover myriads of new worlds, but they are all substantially like our own, and the beyond is still not found. It may, by the natural laws of the natural world, trace cause and effect back and back, even to what it may call the great first cause, which it may name God; but it is a deaf and blind and heartless God, merely an all-pervading principle, controlled by necessity, having no volition, no personality. In this great first cause the natural intellect finds no conscious existence, no power to think, or feel, or love, or will, or consciously to act. In short, no amount of research by the natural intellect, so far as now developed, can discover a personal God, or learn anything of his disposition towards men.

Again, no amount of scientific study, with any data now at the command of science, could ever discover spirit, spiritual existence, spiritual life, nor the laws or conditions of such life.

Science may decompose the human body,—it may most minutely examine all its tissues, all its solids and liquids, its brains and nerves, its heart, its blood, its everything; but it can find no spirit, and no trace of spirit having been there. God and spirit therefore are, for the present at least, beyond the ken of natural science.

The axioms, principles, and corollaries of natural science, as now developed, do not form a basis broad enough on which to erect a tower of sufficient height to give us even a glimpse of spirit or of a personal God. This knowledge is objective; it must come from without,—from beyond the natural world.

Natural man has no means of bridging the abyss between the kingdom of nature and the kingdom whence comes the knowledge of God and spirit. If God would have us possessed of this knowledge, he alone can bridge the abyss and bring it to us on this side of the awful chasm.

We must therefore, I think, conclude a revelation to be necessary:

1. To bring to us a knowledge of the existence of a personal God.

2. To tell us what is needful for us to know of the character of that personal God, and of his disposition towards us.

3. To give us a knowledge of the existence of spiritual life outside of and beyond natural life.

4. To bring to us a knowledge of the fact that man may possess this spiritual life, and its attribute, immortality.

5. To explain to us how and on what conditions man may become possessed of spiritual life, and become heir to immortality.

If God reveals to us things not discoverable by the exercise of our natural faculties, he does it as an act of mercy for our benefit. To be beneficial, it must find a lodgement in our understanding or in our conscious sensibilities, or in both. It must be brought within our comprehension, or to us it is not a revelation. An alleged revelation of something contradictory to our reason, or to our innate sense of justice and right, is not a revelation to our intellects or sensibilities, and consequently is to us no revelation. God in his infinity is beyond the scope of our comprehension. But God's personality, his feelings and designs towards us, and our relations to him, may be brought within our comprehension, and this is about all that we need know from the beyond, and this much we may expect if we have a right to expect anything.

CHAPTER VIII.

Although most of the preceding chapter i not quoted, yet it expresses a fair consensus of the best literature on the subjects treated, at a date a little after the middle of the twentieth century. The best authors sought to impress the public mind, and especially parents and teachers and Christian ministers, with the importance of clearly understanding what man must do for himself, and what God may be expected to do for him. The greatest importance was then attached to the education of the children, and such has been the case ever since on Mars.

This great reform work commenced in the Western World, but it rapidly spread over all parts of the planet.

Creeds largely disappeared, and the improvement of personal character was recognized as the great work of the Christian church. Whatever pertained to this great work commanded the attention of all.

The masses of people had begun to believe there was more for them in their then present life than they had ever been able to grasp, and they eagerly sought a clearer understanding of the conditions necessary to the full enjoyment of that better and more complete life.

We must have an appetite for food if we would properly digest it and have its elements assimilated and converted into blood, flesh, and bones. So a boy must have an appetite for knowledge if his studies are to be assimilated and enter into the composition and growth of his mind. In the same way, it was only when the people of Mars began to hunger and thirst for the better life that they began to grapple with its problems in such a way as to insure their solution and contribute to the healthful growth of society.

As intelligence in this direction increased, a certain kind of selfishness seems to have rapidly decreased. Parents who before had sacrificed their children upon the altars of indolence and fashion and luxury, who, to promote their own selfish ends, had been in the habit of turning their little ones over to ignorant and often corrupt nurses and governesses, now began to understand and appreciate that "as the twig is bent the tree is inclined," that if the best and most was to be obtained from life the preparation for its duties and enjoyments must begin where and when life begins.

Their attention, very early in this awakening, was of course turned to their public and other schools. When so turned, it was discovered that God had been turned out of nearly all these schools. Infidelity and sectarianism had run so high as to excite the jealous fears that one branch of the church would get the advantage of another in its influence over the minds and hearts of the children, and thus bias them in their opinions. This discussion, aided by those opposed to all religions, had resulted in dismissing the Bible from the public schools, and with it all semblance of Christian worship. All religious matter was excluded from the school-books, and even the name of God was not permitted to appear in any such connection as would suggest any accountability to him. In short, the public schools of Mars were godless, and were sending forth swarms of children hardened in profanity, deceit, falsehood, and worse vices. Yet it was to these schools that parents had been invited to look for co-operation in the great work of developing proper character in their children.

The schools seemed to have no regard or care for any part of the child except its intellect, and even this was improperly cared for. The public schools, especially in the Western World, where political equality prevailed, became very

popular, and substantially supplanted all other
schools for primary instruction. This made
the number of children attending these schools
so large as to require the raising by taxation of
large sums of money to defray the expense of
building school-houses, paying teachers, etc.
To restrict this expense to as small an amount
as possible, the schools were graded and classi-
fied, placing under one teacher a large number
of pupils whose attainments were of a similar
grade. These children were taught only in
classes, and class recitations occupied all the
school-hours. This system had its errors, and
very great errors, far-reaching in their evil influence, often entirely thwarting the object of
the schools. The design was intellectual development and culture, while often the result
was to convert a bright, smart, intellectual child
into a stupid, thoughtless dolt, and that too
by the natural, normal working of the system.
The text-books had so systematized the matters
of which they treated as to present the subjects
in natural order, and in such a manner as to
require the mastery and understanding of each
step in the order presented, before being able to
comprehend the next. Children ignorant or
thoughtless of what was before them could not
appreciate the importance of fully understanding these separate steps, each of which was an

important factor in what was to follow. The class was always moving on, regardless of those detained from school from sickness or other causes, regardless also of careless, indolent, or indifferent pupils; and all these, having failed to master the successive steps, could not understand the lessons being taught. When a child was unable to understand his lesson, he would always try to prepare for recitations by memorizing processes, definitions, etc., but in a short time memory failed to serve a student sufficiently to enable him to make creditable recitations. He then fell behind and became discouraged. The system made no provision for him. There was no opportunity for him to have any individual instruction, to bridge him over his troubles.

In a class of thirty or more pupils, grading the same at the beginning of a term, one would be very bright and intellectual, capable of doing all and much more than required; another, naturally dull and stupid, was incapable of doing half what was expected of the class. The balance of the class would range at various points between these two. The extent of the lessons was determined by the average capabilities of the class. The class system compelled holding back the more brilliant, and dragging along too rapidly the duller of even the majority, while the foot of the class was soon dropped back to a lower grade or out of the school. The wings of real genius were constantly being clipped, while wings were attempted to be forced upon those not sufficiently developed to begin to fly. At best, the class instruction could only keep its eye on the middle of the class, holding back the head, and whipping up or dropping off the rear. Society could not afford to lose the real geniuses of its rising generation, nor could it afford to lose the intellectual culture and training of those less brilliant than the medium. In other words, society could not afford to support schools to establish by education a mediocrity, by cutting off those too long and stretching out those too short.

Another evil of the class system was one not easy to avoid. Children would soon form the habit of looking upon the recitation and examination as the sole end and aim of study. They did not study so much to know, as they did to recite creditably. This led to a habit of cramming and forcing, which was morally hurtful, and not conducive to proper intellectual culture. The exclusively class system was a failure, and it became a serious question whether it was not doing more harm than good.

Another evil of the schools had been the effort to teach too much. The people at one time seem to have thought that children must learn in the schools all they would need to know in after-life. Often children were required to carry along five or six studies at the same time. They attempted so much that few could be thorough in anything. This practice of learning a little about a great many things was at one time very fashionable. A little of the nomenclature of the science would often enable one to talk about it, and to make a show of knowledge which he did not possess. Such persons often had indistinct ideas *about* many things, but really *knew* nothing. The mind was found incapable of taking a large number of studies at the same time and really mastering any of them. They found that two studies, thoroughly mastered and understood, did much more to properly develop and cultivate the intellect than many studies only partially understood. The habit of being contented with only a smattering was belittling and demoralizing to the intellect and the character.

They discovered another defect in their educational system. The benefits of their school instruction were limited to childhood and youth. This limitation caused the effort to force upon pupils more knowledge of science than they could possibly comprehend, and so occupied their time and energies as to leave them no opportunity or inclination to learn any industrial pursuits,—no opportunity to discover and cultivate in themselves any adaptiveness for any special business or calling. Many were graduated from these schools as they arrived at the age of manhood and womanhood with no knowledge whatever that fitted them for self-support, and generally with a distaste for such knowledge. They were not educated for the duties of life,—but, on the contrary, their education destroyed their taste for such duties.

The people of Mars finally gained a better idea of education and of the proper use to make of the schools. The child was possessed of certain natural intellectual faculties. It was the office of the school to train the child to the proper control of these faculties. Studentship came to be regarded as a kind of apprenticeship, and the school-room the workshop where the child was to learn how to use his mind,— how to control and direct it in the acquisition of knowledge and the solution of subtle problems, not of science only, but of society and life. Accuracy and thoroughness were essential in every step of such apprenticeship, if one was to become an accepted workman. They learned that accurate thinking begat an appetite for learning,—that when one had the intellectual ability to investigate and understand the propositions of science, religion, civil polity, sociology, etc., and to solve the problems arising therein, such ability always begat an insatiable desire for knowledge of facts and data on which to act, and its possessor was certain to become learned.

The schools and colleges then began to assume their true place in social economy. They began to understand that their office was to make the mind, not merely to disseminate intelligence farther than they could use the intelligence as an instrument in mind-making. When they reached this point, and began to regard the work of the school as done when the student had learned to control and direct his own faculties and had obtained an appetite for learning, they reached the acme of their usefulness. They discovered that when a student had found and been put fully in possession of himself, the schools had done their full duty to him. The balance of the work of becoming learned he could do for himself better than the schools could do it for him.

When men had thus learned how to control and direct their own faculties, and possessed a healthy taste for learning, then better methods of thinking and investigation came into common use, and men became more logical and philosophical. Under such education pedantry could find no place to stand. Pretence and show became transparent and shrank out of sight, and thoughfulness and thoroughness became almost universal, and pervaded all the walks and occupations of life.

In this way the school greatly contributed to the wonderful civilization now existing on Mars. By many generations of such teaching, the intellectual faculties have become more orderly and more under self-control. Children there now possess by heredity such control of their faculties as formerly required a full college course to attain.

The power of attention now possessed by the people of Mars is something astonishing. They seem to possess the ability to direct the mind to the investigation of a subject, and absolutely to dismiss from it, for the time being, everything else. The attention seems to be completely under control of the will. Consequently, all seem to be capable of solving for themselves almost any question that comes up before them. Even with us, we know that the difference in the intellectual power of different minds consists very largely in the difference in power to control the attention. One can hold his mind steadily and continuously on a subject, while another cannot. Almost any mind is powerful when concentrated and held upon one thing. If a powerful sun-glass is focussed on almost any object and held there, the object must dissolve before it; but if the glass is constantly moving, so that the focus is constantly changed, the object will scarcely be warmed. So with the mind: if it can be focussed on a problem and held there, few problems can long resist solution; but, if the mental focus is allowed to vibrate about the question, it will long remain unanswered. Mental conclusions are rarely satisfactory unless they are the result of concentrated thought.

As denominationalism began to disappear, the school-room doors began to open to religious influence, and God began to be recognized in the schools as the source of authority and good government. God and Christian literature came back into the school-books, and a better moral tone and influence came from the school-rooms.

In time people tired of exclusive class instruction in graded schools. While class instruction was continued, much as before, yet every school-room was provided with an additional teacher, whose sole duty was to give individual instruction. The very best teachers were employed in these positions. If a pupil was falling behind his class, losing his interest, or, in the expressive language of slang, "losing his grip," his teacher would invite him into a room separate for that purpose, and by skilful questioning and examination would discover the real cause of trouble, and would generally find it to be a failure to understand some previous link or step in the subject of study. But, whatever the cause, the individual teacher would be almost certain to discover it, and then render such aid as would supply the lost links and reinstate the pupil in his own confidence and to his place in the class.

If the more brilliant pupil of the class was being discouraged or injured by being held back by the slow progress of the class, the individual teacher would aid him in bridging the distance between him and the next higher class, when he would be transferred and given adequate opportunity for the full use of his faculties.

It will be readily understood that none but the most skilful teachers could fill these places. None other would be likely to find the true cause of trouble with pupils, and, having found it, none other would be able to remove it.

They also discovered that there was no good reason for limiting the benefits of school instruction to childhood and youth. On the contrary, it came to be well understood that less study and more manual labor should be urged upon youth, and less manual labor and more study upon manhood. The intellectual faculties of the people of Mars do not decay in old age,

but grow stronger and clearer up to death.
The reason for this is found in the fact that all
are students during their whole lives, and most
of them receive school instruction. The hours
of instruction are so arranged that people may
attend them with very little interference with
hours of labor and business, and when any one
thinks that he has mastered any one subject in
the arts or sciences, he may be examined and
take a certificate or diploma indicating his pro-
ficiency; and thus much valuable time is spent
in study that was formerly spent in idleness,
gossiping clubs, saloons, gambling-halls, and so
forth.

Thus improved the schools became and still
are great aids in the march of mankind towards
a perfect manhood.

Their books indicate that, about the middle
of the twentieth century, their more advanced
thinkers in the field of educational thought and
training hit upon another important idea.
Mankind there, as here, are imitative beings.
They always build after models, real or ideal,
—perhaps always ideal. A landscape-painter
attempts to copy a real landscape, but really
copies his ideal of it. So an artisan, when
building a house or machine, first builds it in
his mind. If his mental conception, his ideal,
is imperfect, his work must be imperfect when

finished. So in character and life: if a child has a false conception of true character, true life, it cannot be expected that he will have a well-proportioned and well-rounded character, nor the most useful and happy life. No one will build better than his ideal.

Parents and teachers on Mars lay great stress on this matter. No feature of a child's education is dwelt upon with more care and perseverance. Every possible effort is made to aid children in getting perfect ideals. The imagination, the ideal-forming faculty, or the inventive faculty, is most carefully and systematically cultured. They have found that, if this faculty is early and persistently trained and brought under the control of the will, impure and corrupting as well as imperfect ideals may be excluded from the mind. They hold that in determining the destiny of a person no faculty of the mind has more to do than the imagination. They have but little hope for a person who has not been trained to hold the imagination under control of the will.

The success of this kind of care and education for many ages past is now seen in the perfection of all their work, and in the beautiful and pure characters met everywhere and in almost every person.

Another subject which received much attention in the education of children was their

emotional natures. Early in the educational
reforms, after the abolition of sectarianism,
thinking men came to see the dangers and evils
of uneducated and untrained emotions. A systematic effort was made by parents and teachers
(principally by parents) so to discipline the
emotional faculties as to bring them under control of the will, and, after several generations
of persistent training and education in that
direction, success crowned their efforts. Uncontrolled emotions were regarded as hurtful to
the health of the body and mind, as well as of
the moral and spiritual natures. Emotional
excesses, even of joy, were injurious in their
direct, and still more so in their reactionary,
effects. When uncontrolled, they made all the
actions of the mind uncertain and unreliable.
They saw that uncontrolled emotions controlled
the will, and that a mind controlled and driven
by the emotions had a crazy guide, more unsta-
ble than the wind. They also saw that the
emotions, when disciplined and under control of
the will, warmed everything they touched, and
added zeal and earnestness and sincerity to all
that one thought or did. To this absolute sub-
jection of the emotions to a well-trained will
is largely due the evenness of temper and the
entire self-control of the people of Mars. They
are never excitable, yet never stoical.

The educationists also made a thorough study of the will, to learn how to subject it to control. The will, being the executive of the mind, needs itself to be trained and disciplined and educated for its work.

I was much interested to know how the people of Mars educated the will,—to know how they succeeded in securing such habits of persistent perseverance in whatever was undertaken, such absolute control of all their appetites and passions, and yet with so little conflict, so little interference with their pleasant relations in their social and personal intercourse with each other, and be so ready to compromise any and all real differences. I had been in the habit of regarding persons of strong will-power as too dictatorial and domineering to be agreeable,—too prone to be officious, to be insinuating their advice or direction where it was not sought or wanted. But on Mars persons of the greatest amount of determination, of apparently the most indomitable wills, would always listen to reason with a seeming entire willingness and desire that the better judgment should rule. There seemed to be no disposition to force the will of one upon another. They would seek to convince the judgment of each other by all proper and legitimate arguments, and they would argue and listen with the sole desire of learning the exact truth. But each was left entirely free, with no ill will or displeasure, to form his own judgment and act in accordance therewith.

Freedom of thought and action—hence freedom of the will—was as nearly absolute as possible in organized society,—free to think and act just as one pleased, so long as such thinking and acting did not violate the like right of others.

I was soon satisfied that wills so docile and orderly, and at the same time so positive and determined, did not come from mere chance and good luck, but must be the result of design and plan. I therefore examined their educational publications in search for their theory of will-education. These books are published for parents and nurses and governesses as well as teachers, and several such volumes were found in every family library. Every such work has a chapter on the education of the will, and there seems to be no radical difference between the methods presented by the different authors. One work seemed to be more popular than the others, as in all the libraries it bore evidence of being most consulted. From this work I make the following extract :

"The will differs from the other faculties of the mind in that it cannot be much educated by the study of science, history, language, etc. Many have regarded the will as a function of the various mental faculties, rather than as itself a faculty, and there is much reason for this opinion. It is not important, however, to discuss this question now, as for our present purpose it matters not whether the will is a mental faculty or whether it is a function of all the faculties.

"The word 'education,' in its ordinary signification, is hardly applicable to the schooling of the will. The words 'train,' 'discipline,' etc., are the better words to use. A child's will may be trained to act in the light of judgment and conscience, rather than by impulse derived from the emotional nature. Or, if the impulse comes from the emotional nature, the will may be trained to refuse to put the impulse into action until approved by judgment and conscience. What is secured by training, to be worked into the character, must be made a habit. If we would have the child grow up in possession of a strong, determined will, and yet one not offensive to others or difficult for others to associate and work with, it involves so many of the mental faculties and so much of the habits of these faculties that the training must begin when these faculties are very young,—in fact, when they are first budding into existence.

The child must form the habit in childhood of
doing just what ought to be done and as it
ought to be done. The child cannot *do* until
it *wills*, and, by careful guarding, it can be
guided to will to do what is right and best,
and then be encouraged and directed in carrying
it to completion, without change or hesitation.
At first, of course, the mother or the nurse
must supply both judgment and will for the
child, yet the habit is being formed. If the
mother is faithful and conscientious, she will be
careful that judgment and conscience are well
consulted in whatever she does for the child,
and everything she causes the child to do, re-
membering that every day adds to the habits
of the child,—habits which will go far to put
the will under control of the appetites and
passions, or of the judgment and conscience.
Many children first awaken to self-consciousness to find their wills already enslaved to appetites and the emotions, to find their passions
turbulent and uncontrolled, and disorder reigning supreme through their whole nature.

"Up to the time the child awakens to consciousness, the will and judgment and conscience
of the parent must supply the place of these
faculties in the child. If they are properly
exercised by the parent, the child comes to consciousness with its faculties developing and

trained in an orderly manner, each performing its own functions in the proper and best way and at the proper time.

"Formerly no systematic effort at education and training was attempted until after the child reached self-consciousness. Up to that age less care was bestowed upon the habits of children than upon puppies and kittens. The child was either neglected or over-attended, indulged or denied, with no reference whatever to the future character of the child, but simply to comply with the state of feelings or whims for the time being of the mother or nurse. The mother knew that if the puppy was to have good habits it must never form bad ones, but she failed to recognize the fact that the same was true of her children.

"It is difficult to account for such indifference of parents as to the earliest habits of their children. Those who, by design or good luck, were fed as, and at such times as, good health demanded, those who were neither rewarded nor punished through the appetite, those who early, *very* early, learned to submit to wholesome parental authority properly exercised, reached the period of consciousness with well-ordered faculties, ready to begin responsible life even-handed, having the emotional nature subordinated to the will, and the will advised and

directed by the judgment and understanding
and conscience. Those children who fell into
the hands of parents who neglected their early
infancy, pampered their appetites, stuffed their
stomachs to produce drowsiness and sleep, then
allayed irritability by cramming with cordials
and sedatives, until the appetite ceased to be an
index of any natural or real want,—making
cheerful submission to parental authority almost
an impossibility, causing a constant and irri-
tating conflict between parents and child, leaving observers to wonder which was first in
authority,—such children reached the period of
self-consciousness with all their faculties dis-
ordered, the judgment and understanding and
conscience exercising no supervision or control,
the passions turbulent and dictatorial, the appetites strong and in full control of the will,
ready to begin responsible life loaded down
with a crushing weight of evil tendencies, and
with all the mental faculties enervated or strong
only for evil.

"The culture of the will, therefore, embraces
almost every other culture. Every faculty of
the mind must be tutored in relation to the
will, or to willing, and the habits of having
the will advised and directed by the higher
mental faculties must be formed very early,
even while these faculties in the parent are

acting for the child, and before the child is old enough to recognize and voluntarily assert its own existence. The old idea that the child must rule the household, and be a tyrannical ruler at that, is all wrong. Before a child is old enough to assert, even by action, its temper and demands, it is old enough to learn to submit to wholesome authority, and must be made to do so if it is to become a useful member of organized society.

" The habits that go to make up the man are what constitute his character. Correct willing, industry, application, zeal, persistence, perseverance, etc., are all subjects of habit. If the man is to possess these sterling and necessary elements of a successful life, the boy must cultivate them as habits, so that they will assert themselves without effort and become commanding and controlling in all he does."

It is clearly apparent that the people of Mars long ago recognized the fact that " the boy is the father of the man" and " the girl is the mother of the woman ;" so their great reforms began with the boys and girls, and have ever since continued there.

CHAPTER IX.

THE ideas advanced in the preceding chapters took root first on the Western Continent of Mars, and grew most rapidly there. The Eastern Continent was divided up into many small governments, with no natural boundaries. Each one was ambitious to extend its boundaries and increase its relative strength by decreasing the size of its neighbors. This policy, which held sway for more than twenty centuries, demanded large standing armies, and immense expenditures for fortifications and armament. These armies, even in times of peace, required the service of every able-bodied man for a considerable portion of his mature life. Thus was the attention of the governments and the people distracted from any plans or efforts for ameliorating the condition of the common people. The able-bodied men being in the armies, and substantially without recompense except food and clothing, the support of the family at home fell almost entirely upon the mothers and daughters. They tilled the soil and gathered the crops, and even worked

at the forge and in the machine-shops and
other shops and factories. The children were,
of necessity, left without mental or moral culture, except what they got at the schools after
arriving at school age. That period of the
child's life when the best and worst habits were
formed was almost entirely left to luck and
chance. After the men had spent from five
to eight years in the armies in times of peace,
most of the time in the idleness of camp life,
they had contracted habits of indifference and
indolence, rarely afterwards overcome. Hence
there prevailed such a want of enterprise and
manly spirit as kept them content with their
degraded and miserable condition, and made
it possible for the few to absorb all the good
things of life and to rule the men with rods
of iron.

What little inventive genius had developed
under these adverse circumstances was almost
entirely directed to creating and improving
engines of war. Implements for destroying
property and human life were brought to great
perfection. Explosives of tremendous power
for destruction were invented. Towns and
cities could be destroyed from a distance of ten
miles away. Torpedo-boats were constructed
which could be sent under water a distance of
eight or ten miles, and unerringly plant the

torpedoes charged with such explosives under the sides of the largest vessels, causing instant destruction of vessels and crews. Machine-guns were invented, with which two brave and skilful men could hold a position against a charging column of many thousands.

These and many other terrible engines of destruction led the people of Mars, about the beginning of the twentieth century, to consider, more earnestly than they had ever done before, the question of settling international disputes without wars. It was found that it mattered not how ingenious or efficient were the means of attack, skilful means of defence were immediately invented to meet them, so that what was the best one year was abandoned as worthless the next. New naval vessels, new fortifications and armaments, were constantly being devised and constructed, making taxation and expenditures absolutely crushing, even in the richest nations.

The governments in the Western World more generally had natural boundaries, and were much less ambitious to extend them. They felt abundantly able to defend their soil against foreign encroachments. They possessed much more inventive genius than the Eastern World, and their artisans were more rapid in constructing work put into their hands; consequently they made no serious attempt to keep abreast of the Eastern World in implements of war, preferring to trust to the genius and skill of their inventors and artisans to provide means of assault and defence, should occasion require. Hence, without fear of being charged with cowardice, they could and did first propose measures for settling international disputes without resort to arms. These measures were discussed by the people of all the civilized and semi-civilized nations of the planet, and generally with so much favor as to result, after a few years, in the calling of a convention of two commissioners from each and every nation that might desire to be represented therein.

Almost all the civilized nations sent representatives to this convocation. The convention was in session nearly two years, and finally resulted in an agreement upon a kind of international constitution, to be binding upon such nations as might subscribe to the same. This constitution had many excellent provisions. Among them were the following, in substance:

1. That an international congress should be organized, in which each nation signing the constitution should be entitled to two members, the members holding their positions subject to the will of the nations sending them, except

that, for unparliamentary conduct, or conduct calculated to bring the congress into disrepute, any member might be expelled by a two-thirds vote of the congress; and any person once expelled could never again become a member, except by the consent of the congress expressed by a like vote.

2. That the congress should be in perpetual session. To make this practicable, it was provided that on all questions before the congress each nation should be entitled to but one vote. If its two delegates were present and could not agree, then the vote should be cast by the one oldest in commission. To provide for this, the commissions of no two delegates from the same nation should bear the same date. This arrangement admitted of one-half the delegates being absent without interrupting the proceedings. So the members could have all necessary vacations, with no vacation in the sessions of the congress.

3. That all matters of international dispute which could not otherwise be amicably settled should be submitted to this congress, where the same should be fully considered, upon such evidence as the disputing nations might see fit to present. This testimony could be submitted to a committee or to the congress in regular session, as the congress might decide. Each disputant

should be allowed to appear before the congress by attorney, if it so desired, when the matter should be fully considered and decided by a majority vote. All questions thus decided became irrevocable decrees, binding upon both and upon all nations concerned.

4. That the constitution should be considered in the nature of a treaty, offensive and defensive, between all the nations which were parties to it.

5. That, if any nation whose cause of complaint had been submitted to and decided by the congress should refuse to abide by and obey such decision or decree, then such nation should cease to be represented in the congress, and all the other nations represented should withdraw their diplomatic representatives from, and cease all communications with, such refractory nation and its people, and all the commercial relations with its people should cease until such time as said nation should set itself right before the nations, and make the proper *amende honorable*, after which its delegates might again become members of the congress.

6. In case any outside nation should declare war against any member of the compact, unless such member should by the congress be considered clearly wrong, and as having given just cause for such declaration, in the light of inter-

national law, such outside nation should be considered as an outlaw by all nations belonging to the compact, and be treated as pirates, and it should be considered as proper cause for dismissal from the compact for any of its members to render any aid to such piratical nation.

It was also provided that, in case of any dispute between any member of the compact and any other nation not a member, the member might submit its cause *ex parte* to the congress for its judgment and advice, and, if such member followed the judgment of the congress, it should have the aid and sympathy of all the other members.

7. That the constitution might be amended, by embodying the desired amendment in a resolution, which should receive a majority vote of the congress, after which it should lie over for one year, and be submitted to all the nations belonging to the compact, allowing such nations opportunity to instruct their representatives. After the expiration of one year, the amendment could become a part of the constitution by a two-thirds vote of the congress.

8. That no nation belonging to the compact should go to war with any other nation, whether a member or not, without consent of the congress.

9. That every nation belonging to the com-

pact should use its influence to promote peace
and dispel the war-spirit all over the planet.

10. That the constitution should go into
force when five nations should sign the same
and commission their representatives to the
congress.

Nearly all the leading governments approved
this constitution at once, and commissioned
their representatives. The weaker governments
soon followed, so that, when the congress assembled, every civilized government was fully
represented. The half-civilized soon followed.
Delegates also appeared from all tribes and
peoples that had made any considerable progress
towards civilization. The applications of all
were duly considered, and, if it was found they
represented any real government, whether considered civilized or not, they were admitted.

Questions submitted to the congress were so
justly and so wisely considered and decided,
that the congress became very popular as a
court of supreme judicature for all nations, on
all international questions. The best and ablest
men in each nation were selected, as each felt a
national pride in being ably represented in a
body of such dignity and influence.

Its discussions and decisions were published
in all languages, and read in their own tongue
by all that could read. The people began very

soon to see and understand what trivial matters had caused great wars, and how easily they could be settled without war. A proper apology, if it was a matter of indignity or personal affront, and restitution, if a matter of property, saved a great waste of time and treasure and blood and life. But, after all, the great loss of treasure and blood and life was not the greatest evil of wars. Wars took the minds of the governing classes away from the internal affairs of the nation, and these affairs, and largely of all classes,—such as agriculture, commerce, manufacturing, education, morality, religion, etc.,—were left to struggle without the aid and guidance of the best minds. It was in this way that wars were most effective in retarding the progress of civilization.

The governments continued their armaments on land and sea until they became satisfied that their high international court of judicature had come to stay; then, by common consent, in compliance with a resolution of advice of the international congress, they began the process of disarming, and all the armies and navies of the world were reduced to the number needed as an internal police, to enforce local laws and maintain peace and security at home. Their cannon were moulded into ploughs, and their swords literally beaten into pruning-hooks, and men turned their attention to useful employments.

Not until universal peace was established, and further wars were no longer apprehended, did the people of the nations realize the real and greatest evil of Mars. They had for many centuries concentrated the best talent upon erecting barriers to civilization, obstacles to the best good of mankind. All the spirit and energy and courage and enterprise of the nations had been exhausted in efforts at human destruction. Now that international wars were forever at an end, people of heart and brains turned their attention more to economics and sociology,—to real statesmanship. As they did so, they quickly discovered the spirit of injustice as reigning supreme everywhere. They saw that the few were reaping the products of the labor of the many; that the masses had for many ages, with comparative willingness, consented to be the hewers of wood and the carriers of water for the privileged few; that the few amassed great fortunes and lived in opulent luxury, while all around them were poverty and hunger and distress. The observing and thoughtful could easily see that this condition of things must continually breed discontent, turbulence, and civil wars. An international congress could adjust and settle international disputes, but it could not adjust social and individual wrongs. But the success of the intertional congress in abolishing international wars was a great stimulus to the nations to prevent by peaceable means internal discords, and to remove all causes and dangers of civil wars. Hence all national plans for ameliorating the condition of the common people, and for ridding society of poverty, received respectful and candid consideration.

It was quickly discovered that a very large proportion of the poverty and distress was the result of bad habits, of indulgence, indolence, and wastefulness, and could not be permanently relieved except by a change of these habits. But habits, once formed, are not easily changed. So these statesmen were soon ready to agree with the educationists, that the place to begin was with childhood.

The influence of this congress did not end with the extinction of war. It brought the lowest grades of civilization in contact with the highest, in such way as to lead the uncivilized and half-civilized people to see what they were losing, and induce them to accept the measures best adapted for their improvement. Even as a missionary enterprise the international congress far excelled all that had ever before been done. It was quickly recognized that the Christian nations were much in advance of all the others in everything that contributed to human happiness, and other forms of religion began to give way to Christianity. The nations which manifested the spirit of Christ in securing religious liberty to their people, equality of political rights, and justice between man and man, were most popular and influential in the congress and among the nations, and their institutions and laws and customs and language were most copied by the various people of the planet.

National prejudices began to crumble, and the fraternal spirit began to grow and extend, so that the long-talked-of universal brotherhood of man, which has since been reached on Mars, was distinctly foreshadowed. The congress was a kind of open door through which the nations could see each other more closely than ever before,—could see what to copy and what to avoid.

The men of the Eastern World, being relieved from army life, began to assume the support of their families, and to abandon their habits of indolence and indifference and the vices springing therefrom. The wives and mothers, being relieved from farm and shop service, turned their attention more to their homes and the care and culture of their children. The men soon began to recognize the fact that a large proportion of the product of their labor and genius belonged to themselves, and they became more industrious, ambitious, and spirited. In a few generations men began to be esteemed and respected for their real worth in genius, skill, and character, rather than for the accident of birth or the possession of riches.

After these ideas and influences became prevalent, it was not long before the people ceased being born to rank and position. Rank and position went to those who earned them, thereby putting a premium on industry, culture, and character.

The abolition of laws for the collection of debts placed a premium upon integrity and character. Integrity and common honesty between man and man were more brought into business transactions, and frauds and breaches of trust greatly diminished. This was a great stimulus to parents and teachers in the training of childhood and the building of character.

These laws constituted the first serious legal steps towards making character, instead of wealth, the ticket of admission to social position. Dishonesty, deception, false representations in business, intemperance, extravagance, and profligacy in all its forms, became more hateful and disgraceful than ever before. Idle luxury was disreputable, and lost caste in society. Living in idle luxury upon hoarded wealth was looked upon as a species of dishonesty, and became unpopular. The poor began to understand that much of their poverty and distress was because of idleness, or wastefulness, or intemperance, or other bad habits, or want of skill; and these habits became disgraceful, and want arising from them lost the sympathy and help of better people. This stimulated them to correct their own habits and look much more closely to the habits of their children.

Through the international congress and the publications incident to it, these ideas spread rapidly over the world, and soon began to take root everywhere.

CHAPTER X.

In the twentieth century a decided reform was inaugurated, ending in changing and greatly improving the rights of property in lands. In most of the eastern countries the land was parcelled out in large tracts to a favored few, who held the same in perpetuity, passing the titles from father to oldest son through the generation. These landlords would divide up their possessions into small holdings, to be occupied, improved, and cultivated by tenants. The greed of landlords would allow little or nothing for necessary improvements, but always demanded a large share of the products of these holdings as rentals, which, together with the government taxes, always kept the tenants in a condition of dependence, and made them suppliants at the feet of their masters, the landlords. In this way the landlords throttled the common people, and choked out of them their personal independence, their manly spirit, their ambition and enterprise. This land-system had for centuries been a barrier to any high state of civilization, and ultimately became a cause of great discontent, leading to turmoil and insurrections, and greatly threatened the stability of governments.

In the Western World the cultivated land was generally owned by those who occupied and cultivated it. The unoccupied land mostly belonged to the governments, and was sold, with few restrictions, in parcels to suit purchasers, at little more than nominal prices. As the population increased, and the public lands were being rapidly absorbed, a greed seems to have been developed among capitalists to acquire large tracts of these lands, with intent to hold them until the arable public lands should all be sold, when they could command greatly advanced prices. This anxiety for large landed possessions became common all over the country. Wealthy farmers would enlarge their farms by buying out and dispossessing their neighbors, often enlarging them far beyond their ability to cultivate, so that it was common to see large fields, that had been under high cultivation, neglected and lapsing again to a wild state.

Early in the twentieth century the dissatisfaction with the various systems of land-tenure was almost universal all over the planet. It was argued by very many that every one born into the world had a right to standing-room, working-room, and living-room, and that this right was not compatible with the rights of a few to monopolize and appropriate to their own use the whole surface of the planet.

The remedies presented to the public for the real and apprehended evils of systems of land-ownership were numerous. Some urged, with many plausible arguments, that the government should confiscate all the land and hold it for the common use, claiming that every one born into the world had the same right to the free use of the land as he had of the air and water, and that no man should be permitted to fence in a portion of it and call it his own and transmit it to his children and his children's children.

The more thoughtful, however, while recognizing the evil of landlordism, could see no rational remedy in the doctrine of confiscation. They then began to devise means to make it unprofitable for a man to own more land than he could profitably cultivate. Various ways for doing this were advocated. Some urged very persistently that all taxes, of whatever kind, should be levied upon and collected from the land. This, it was thought, would deter many from holding uncultivated lands, and would lead to better land-distribution. Others saw that this would be oppressive to small farmers. It was putting the whole burden of the government upon the producers of the necessaries of life.

Finally laws were enacted taxing most heavily unoccupied lands, thereby making it unprofitable and undesirable to hold lands to secure the advance in prices caused by surrounding occupancy and culture. This was followed by making it illegal for any one person to hold more than a prescribed amount of land. A certain amount could be held by or for each person who might desire to occupy and cultivate it. The head of a family might buy and occupy this amount for each and all of its members, provided he properly cultivated it.

In this way, by gradual advances, the land was ultimately divided up into comparatively small lots, and no injustice was done to anybody. The lots were sufficient in size, if properly cultivated, to furnish adequate support for the occupants. As population increased, the inventive faculties of the people were stimulated to devise new methods of increasing the fertility of the soil, and improving the quality as well as the quantity of production. From time to time, as population became more and more dense, the amount of land-holding *per capita* was diminished, yet leaving enough for all desiring to till the soil. Down to the present time, increased fertility of the soil, and improved methods of culture, have caused the increased production of the soil to keep pace

15*

fully with the increase of population, and there
is no fear felt of a population beyond the ca-
pacity of the planet to house, clothe, and feed.
The people have full faith that man's inventive
faculties will continue to meet all demands and
emergencies.

To reach this condition of land-distribution
required centuries of trial and struggle, and
much turmoil and bloodshed. It was not, in
fact, reached until considerable advance was
made in the classification of society; not until
the possession of riches ceased to be the card
of admission to social standing; not until character, real personal worth, became the measure
of a man's personal influence and the index
of his social position. At this time the selfish
grasp of unneeded property began to relax its
hold, and a sense of justice, of what was right
between man and man, began to prevail. When
this sense began to sway and rule men's actions,
each one recognized the existence of a natural
law of brotherhood,—that the highest good of
each depended largely upon the highest good
of all, and "live and let live" became an accepted law. It was recognized that in one
sense society was unitary,—that, as in the
human body no portion of it could suffer without affecting the whole body, so in society, in
the great body-politic, no portion of it could

be in distress without every other portion of it being injured by that distress. The degrading influences of poverty, and the debauching influences of luxury, were alike destructive to the highest aspirations of all. When these truths were clearly discerned, and the good of each was sought in promoting the good of all, then social wrongs were rapidly righted.

It was found that everything depended on the restoration of the sense of justice to its umpirage in human transactions.

CHAPTER XI.

One of the most interesting things that attracted my attention on Mars was what, to me, was a new power, which all seemed to possess, but in different degrees. What this power was, or how obtained, I was unable fully to understand. Persons seemed to exercise it on things beyond reach, without any perceptible medium. It seemed to be a power of the human will, by means of which the will moved and controlled things external to the person, with almost the same facility that it moved the hand, the tongue, or the foot. It was a power constantly used in all kinds of labor, and seemed almost entirely to relieve the people from the fatigue of labor. The only fatigue seemed to arise from the close, intense attention that was demanded for the best effects. Very many mechanical devices had been invented to utilize to the best advantage this wonderful power, and new inventions are constantly being made for a like purpose. To a very great extent it was used in place of manual, horse, and steam power. Some seemed to be much more skilled in its use than others. Occasionally one was met who was almost entirely destitute of it. I was assured that in some rare instances persons had lost this power who once possessed it in a high degree.

This power seemed to be a purely psychic force, but to me it was occult, and its exercise miraculous. I had before witnessed some inexplicable exhibitions of what was called mesmerism. But these exhibitions had been crude and unsatisfactory. While the mesmerists seemed able to exhibit a new force, yet the force was erratic and unreliable, subject to no known laws. But on Mars the psychic force was an ordinary willpower, subject to the same laws and control as other actions of the will. The people there protested that there was nothing miraculous or supernatural about it. They cited the first commandment in their Bible, "Thou shalt multiply and replenish the planet *and subdue it.*" They said that "to subdue it" meant to master the principles of nature, discover its laws, and harness them into the service of man. This to a considerable extent they claimed to have done already, and they are constantly making new discoveries, and securing from nature additional services because of such discoveries.

On Mars, as on the Earth, scholarly men are unfriendly to the idea that an omniscient and omnipotent God would need, under any cir-

m

cumstances, to interrupt the natural workings of his own laws or to work through those laws irregularly. To such persons a miracle, as commonly understood, is repulsive, tending to belittle one's idea of God. The people of Mars believe that Christ did no miracles, in the common signification of the word "miracle." They admit and believe that Christ did what the Gospels say he did, but claim that there was nothing supernatural about these works. They believe that Christ, being from his nature thoroughly conversant with all the principles and laws of nature, and having perfect control of this psychic force, did, by the application of this force to the principles and laws of nature, perform his wonderful works.

This, they claim, does not subtract from the dignity or power of Christ, but rather adds thereto.

On Mars it is believed that man will yet be able to do all the wonderful works that Christ did. Christ, when among men, said, " Verily, verily, I say unto you, He that believeth on me, the works that I do shall he do also,—and greater works shall he do." It is believed that, as man increases his wisdom and virtue, as he cultivates more and more the spirit of Christ, and studies more and more deeply into the laws of physical nature and into the mental and moral nature of man, he will greatly increase his power over nature, and will be able easily and daily to accomplish what in earlier times were regarded as miracles.

This psychic force is applied everywhere where force is needed. When many join together, and exert their wills in the same direction, the force developed becomes enormous, and is used for many practical purposes. They even feel confident that, by aid of this force, and a further knowledge of the laws relating to meteorology, which they are now carefully investigating, they will be able to control the winds and produce dry weather and rains at pleasure. I learned that only those who were entirely free from any taint of disease of either body or mind, acquired or inherited, and whose intellectual, emotional, and spiritual natures were evenly developed, so as to be entirely under the control of the conscience and judgment, possessed control of this psychic force in a high degree, and that they may lose it by a loss of purity and integrity.

In their scientific and philosophic studies and investigations they have gone far beyond us in every department of knowledge. Much that is speculation and hypothesis with us, is fixed science with them. Their inherited intellectual and moral strength and development are such that they grapple questions with a vigor and strength unknown to us. Our strongest and clearest intellects here are only a prophecy of what is common there. Their great unity of doctrine and practice is the result of their accurate knowledge. Here it is understood that differences of opinion arise either from prejudice or imperfect knowledge, and that honest study must diminish such differences. The more men think and study, in an honest search for truth, the nearer will their opinions coincide. There they have advanced so far in honest research that all are agreed on many questions that now greatly divide us. Yet with them knowledge has its boundaries, and on the outskirts, where their knowledge is imperfect, differences of opinion exist. But they have long since learned to exercise in this great charity and liberality, knowing that further research will bring all together. So, between science and religion there are no feuds. Theology no longer opposes itself to science, and science does not arrogate to itself the right to question the truths of theology. Men are left free and encouraged to seek truth in every field of knowledge, with no fears whatever that these truths when discovered will be unfriendly to each other. The intellect and the moral nature, science and theology, the material and the spiritual, are all recognized as God's books, and the truths of all these books are God's truths and cannot conflict with each other. All apparent contradictions are only exhibitions of imperfect knowledge, and will disappear as the knowledge becomes clear and perfect. When truths are fully seen and understood, they must always coincide and harmonize with one another.

Another very noticeable thing among the people of Mars was their wonderful power of insight into each other, especially between intimate friends. Those who lived in confidential relations seemed to be almost transparent to each other. This was so noticeable as to excite in me great wonder, and lead me to suspect that here was another power which I had not before known, but I was assured that such was not the case. As an explanation of this power, I was cited to a paragraph in an old book, written several centuries ago. It reads as follows : " It is well known how readily two persons, of generous, confiding natures, will blend together when brought for a considerable time into intimate relations with each other. Each seems to be an open book to the other. They can read each other's thoughts and feelings with almost unerring certainty. But let either get even a suspicion that the other is

16

insincere, and seeking to use him for selfish purposes, and how quickly they draw out from each other! Close the books, and to each other they become opaque. Selfishness separates people and makes them mysteries to each other. Selfishness is always insincere, and always shuts one up within himself. It closes all avenues of confidential relationship between man and man, and is incompatible with the highest and truest friendship. It makes each seek to hide his real self from the other. If men could become unselfish, a generous confidence would become universal, and mind and mind, and heart and heart, would so blend together as to enable each to read the other as if an open book. While selfishness is so universal, men are opaque to each other and unreadable. Before mankind can rise to their highest estate, even as mankind, men must be able to affiliate in such a way as easily to understand each other, and with ability so to read each other as to make deception next to impossible. This condition of social intercourse can come only when man seeks his happiness in promoting the happiness of others; when he ceases trying to build himself up by tearing others down,— ceases becoming rich by making others poor; when the sense of justice becomes strong and controlling: then associated efforts in any good

cause will become a powerful, almost an irre-
sistible effort."

The people of Mars, through their many
centuries of careful training and education,
have attained the condition suggested in the
foregoing paragraph. No one seems to think
of finding happiness amid surrounding misery;
so the energies of all are directed to promoting
the good of all, and mutual trust and confidence seem to be universal. Every one seems
to aim at lightening the burdens of his neighbor. The sick and unfortunate are kindly
cared for, without intermediate societies or
almshouses. They are cared for without being
made to feel that they are paupers. Aid, when
necessary, is bestowed without destroying the
self-respect of the recipient.

The persistent culture of many centuries has
fully developed the sense of justice which had
only an embryotic existence before. Now no
trait of character is stronger or more universal.
Each measures out to the other all that is justly
and honorably due in every deal. There are
no attempts to overreach each other by the use
of any kind of deception. "It is naught, it is
naught, saith the buyer; but when he is gone
his way, he boasteth," is no longer a proverb
applicable on Mars. No one there exaggerates
the value of a thing because it is his own; no

one depreciates its value because it belongs to another.

They have publications there corresponding to our newspapers, but they are remarkable for the absence of flaming and extolling advertisements. Very little advertising is done. The full extent of it is to notify the public of a trader's name, location, and business. These advertisements have no display, and rarely occupy more than one or two lines. The fences, rocks, and sides of buildings are never disfigured with posters and lithographs. Some old files of newspapers found in their public libraries show that many centuries ago they advertised as we do here ; but experience taught them that it was better to abstain from much advertising, and deduct the cost thereof from the selling price of their goods. The people finally discovered that the purchasers, and not the sellers, were paying the cost of advertising. So there was a popular demand for its abolition.

The advertisements now seen there never extol the advertiser's wares, never compare the price or quality of his goods with those of his neighbor's, but always leave their customers to judge for themselves.

It is taken for granted that people know their own wants, and so no one is urged to buy anything. Goods in the shops are so exposed as to be readily seen by customers, yet there are no magnificent displays, no expensive arrangements merely for the display of goods and wares. In this, as in other things, inexpensive simplicity is the rule of practice, thereby reducing the cost of wares to customers.

Their fully-evolved sense of justice entirely prevents ruinous competition, and the same sense prevents ruinous prices in the absence of competition. Nothing so quickly loses customers to a tradesman as the discovery that he is wanting in this sense.

Another noticeable feature of their newspapers was the absence of all sensational reading-matter. The papers were not printed for depraved appetites and idlers. They were filled with useful news and information. New discoveries in the practical and fine arts were early heralded all over the planet, and fully described. The newspapers were used, largely, by persons of advanced thought, and they were the medium for the dissemination of new and useful knowledge, and even for discussing questions of speculative philosophy. A highly moral and deeply religious sentiment pervaded all articles published in their newspapers as well as in their books. In fact, the religion of Christ was immanent everywhere and in everything on Mars. In their laws, in the execution

16*

of their laws, in their labor-system, in their manufacturing, in their division of profits between capital and labor, in their bartering and trading, in their banking, in their systems for transportation, in their every-day dealings with each other, in their writings, in their discussions, in their politics, in their schools, in their churches, in their social intercourse, in everything and everywhere, the spirit and the teachings of Christ are always recognized and heeded. This was especially noticeable in their newspapers, where all met on common ground and discussed all questions that could in any degree benefit anybody. The newspapers were all published in a form to facilitate preservation, and they were carefully kept for future reference.

In the publication offices the type were all set and distributed by machinery. This machinery was so simple and efficient that a boy or girl sixteen years of age could easily do the work of eight or ten good type-setters by the old method, and that, too, with no more labor or fatigue than is required to run one of our type-writing machines,—simply by fingering the letters upon an ordinary key-board : consequently, the printing of newspapers was accomplished at so little cost that, even without a large income from advertising, good papers could be published and sold at a price within the means of all.

CHAPTER XII.

GOVERNMENT, among the people of Mars, is a very simple, inexpensive affair. Such a people need but little governing. Yet school-houses must be built and schools maintained; their great libraries must be cared for; high-ways must be constructed and kept in repair; necessary taxes must be levied, collected, and disbursed; and many other things, strictly for the public good and convenience, call for the machinery of government, even among a peo-ple so nearly perfect. They have executive, legislative, and judicial departments, in gov-ernments, yet each is more simple in its struc-ture, as the demands for the interference of the government in the affairs of men are small compared to what they are here.

The executive is more like a patriarch than a governor. He watches to see that no dis-turbing causes spring up to molest the peace of society in any part of the commonwealth, and to see that the public burdens are evenly and equitably distributed and borne by the people. He instructs public functionaries as to their duties, and, in general, watches all the public interests of the people.

The legislative department has but little to do. The statutory laws are very few, and most of them very old. Excessive legislation long ago ceased to be the folly of the people of Mars. Reforms were secured by correcting public opinion, rather than by legislation. The statutes are so few, and have been so long maintained without change, that all know and obey them. The time has been there, as here, when statutory laws were very numerous, occupying many large volumes, and a new volume was added every year. Laws then were constantly being made, amended, repealed, re-enacted, etc., so that no one could know them. Many of these laws were ambiguous, and their meaning was quite uncertain until the judicial department had given them a construction. Much of the vast amount of litigation that afflicted the people of those times grew out of excessive legislation and the uncertainty as to what the law was. As men grew better and wiser they repealed more laws than they made, so that the volumes of statutory laws gradually diminished until they reached their present simple condition. When men took no conscience into their business, but felt they could rightfully take any advantage of their fellowmen that statutory law would permit, there was a constant temptation to put the laws into such shape as would facilitate conscienceless schemes.

The judicial department of government on Mars is almost entirely relieved from the disagreeable features of the courts of olden times. There is now very little litigation, and no acrimony or bitterness accompanies it. Men come into court, with or without attorneys, as they please, when an honest difference exists between them as to their relative rights. All they desire is what is just and proper, whether technically legal or not. So, often the court becomes more of an arbiter between friends than a strictly judicial tribunal. It is the business of courts and attorneys to prevent disputes and differences, rather than to court and cultivate them. Attorneys are popular in proportion as they keep disputants out of the courts, and cultivate friendship between them. Hence trial dockets are short, and litigation occupies very little time of the courts.

The courts are institutions that have come down from olden times, having less and less to do, as civilization has advanced, and men have approached nearer and nearer the status of the perfect man. The sense of justice has been so highly evolved in the hearts of the people, there is very little cause for litigation, there

being so little inclination among men to reach
after or attempt to hold what belongs to others.
Fair and honest dealing is so nearly universal as
to make public indignation a sufficient punishment to one who would seek to violate the rule.

It would seem that the courts might be entirely abolished with but little danger to peace
and justice. They would long since have ceased
to exist, but for the fear that their absence
might possibly, at some time, give rise to self-
constituted courts, with their accompanying
irregularities and peace-destroying tendencies.

In the earlier ages, when education was almost monopolized by the priesthood and other
favored few, public opinion was artificially
created by appeals to the superstitions and
brutality of ignorance and heartlessness. Public opinion was then a tyrant, always ready to
cry out, "Crucify him, crucify him!" against
any one who dared to think or act in opposition
to the privileged classes or the dogmas of the
priesthood. In later times, when education
had freed the intellect, and men became able
and willing to do their own thinking, and each
was willing to concede to all others the rights
and privileges he claimed for himself, public
opinion became more humane and just, and
frowned only upon such as abused their privileges by using their liberties to the injury of

others. This public opinion was strong enough in almost all cases to hold in check any hereditary tendency of olden-time selfishness that might occasionally crop out, so that courts were rarely called upon to correct such tendencies.

The aim of all departments of government is to interfere just as little as possible with the affairs of the people. Men have cultivated the habit of self-control to such extent as to require but little aid of organized governments.

The governments on Mars are all based on republican principles, and through the international congress they are so closely allied as almost to constitute a single government. Each is composed of several states, similar to our United States. These separate states, often located in different climates, having different products, and the people different employments, called for the exercise of considerable genius and statesmanship to secure such unity of interest as was necessary to maintain a unity of states.

Their history shows that long ago the nations of Mars passed through a civil-service reform epoch similar to the one through which we are being whirled and shuffled to-day.

At the seats of government large numbers of clerks were always employed in the several departments, to transact the public business. The spirit of reform made a strenuous effort to place these clerical and *quasi*-official positions outside of partisan control. Examining committees were organized, and standards of qualification established, and candidates for position were examined, and professedly appointed, because of certain qualifications, without regard to their party affiliations. These appointees could not be removed except for sufficient cause. But this plan was not successful for several reasons : (1) It was rarely carried out in good faith. (2) If a dozen or more were appointed at a given time, it was found that at least one-half of them would have sufficient spirit and enterprise to find some other occupation more profitable and congenial than that of a mere clerk ; so after a year or two they would resign and leave the places vacant, to be filled in the same way, and a like proportion would again become vacant. Those without spirit and enterprise would content themselves as mere clerks, with no ambition to become anything more. They would be careful to discharge their routine duties just well enough not to give cause for dismissal. In this way it took only a few years to fill all the departments with appointees who had not the ambition and manhood to earn a livelihood anywhere else, and consequently were not desirable even as clerks. (3) The plan tended to build up a class of government dependents. In their sycophantic efforts to be non-partisan, they unmanned themselves, and became little more than nonentities.

The civil-service reform theory presumed that the longer a man held a position the more valuable his service became, but this proved not to be true. In fact, just the reverse was true. The clerks who were content to remain clerks were of the kind to fall into business ruts and become "red-tape winders," and thus were really obstructionists to all business men having anything to do with the departments. It was found that a new clerk, fresh from the busy world outside, would accomplish more in one day than an old clerk would in two, and do it better.

After many changes in the plans and systems of civil service, and much discussion of the subject, they finally adopted the one now in operation, which has for centuries proved eminently satisfactory.

At the seat of every national government there is a great national university, of high order and wide scope. The whole country embraced by a government is divided into districts, corresponding to our congressional districts, divided upon the basis of population. The appointments to clerical and other semi-official positions are equitably apportioned among these

districts, and are given only to such as wish
to become students in the national university.
Applicants are examined for admission to this
institution, and they enter the university and
the civil service simultaneously. The hours
of study and recitation are adapted to the demands of the civil service, and the time to
complete a university course is sufficiently extended to enable diligent students properly to
fill the twofold office of student and clerk. The
salaries of clerks are barely sufficient to defray
their necessary expenses as students. Dismissal
from the university is also a dismissal from the
clerical position, and a dismissal from a clerical
position is also a dismissal from all gratuitous
privileges of the university.

This system works admirably. As the stu-
dent-clerks are appointed from examinations
conducted under the auspices of the universities,
party affiliations have no consideration. It is
presumed that all applicants are desirous of
obtaining an education at the universities, and
this desire stimulates to efficiency as clerks and
to diligence and good conduct as students, for
the loss of one position is the loss of both. It
has been found, too, that a student makes a
better clerk than one who is not a student.
The student's mind is active, and his percep-
tions are quick and clear, and his comprehen-

sion is more reliable; while the mere clerk is almost certain to become comparatively dull, slow, and stupid.

This plan of civil service in the departments at the seats of government has now been in successful operation several centuries, and the good results are seen in all directions. Chronic place-holders are no longer seen in the departments, and the national capitols no longer swarm with government mendicants. Government employment is no longer destructive of genuine manhood, but, on the contrary, is elevating, and fits employees for the best callings in life. A new supply of clerks comes into the departments every year, fresh from the people in all parts of the country, and new supplies of university graduates are sent to all parts. These graduates go home thoroughly familiar with the management and inner working of the government, and disseminate this accurate information among the people. They also by several years' residence at the capital obtain a more accurate knowledge of public men and measures than is possible except by such residence. On returning home, these graduates become authorities on matters of public measures and men, and political tricks are far less possible,—even if there was any disposition among the people to practise them.

Another great benefit derived from the plan is that it proves a strong tie to bind the different sections of a government together. However diverse may be the material products of the different sections of the country, and however different may be the employments of the people, yet their minds and their hearts were moulded together in the same great university, —they worked together, studied together, and matured together,—and thus the university and the civil service bind the sections together with a stronger cord than is found in any other influence. They have built national and international brotherhoods all over the planet, that are great conservators of peace, and good will, and good government.

Minor officers scattered through the country are appointed for a specified term, and very rarely reappointed. Thus great care is taken not to build up an office-holding class, or a class of government dependents. On Mars government is in no sense a lazar-house or infirmary.

As character, personal worth, intelligence, and Christian morality became the tickets of admission to the best society and to positions of great personal influence, wealth became less desirable, and beyond what was needed for comfortable support was not sought. As the

desire for riches diminished, there was no longer
any object in concentrating great wealth; so
large corporations and trusts began to crumble
into pieces, and wealth and population drew
out of cities, and sought more quiet and congenial homes where population was less dense.
This tendency was much encouraged by philanthropists and true reformers. It had long
been known that the most potent agency to
restrain and reform the evil-inclined was public
opinion. But large cities afforded such facilities to escape the public eye, that young people
would often progress so far on a downward
road as to lose self-respect and get beyond the
influence of public opinion before it could be
brought to bear upon them. Dens, and places
calculated to undermine and debauch character,
could hide themselves from public gaze in
large cities as they could not in places more
sparsely populated. The young were often en-
ticed into these places and ruined, before their
friends and neighbors knew that such places
existed.

In all ages there has been a laudable desire,
in almost all, to occupy positions of influence
and trust. When riches constituted the high-
way to such positions, all scrambled to become
rich. Large cities in many ways afforded the
best facilities for the accumulation of wealth,

especially when the few were to become wealthy
by out-witting the many. So dense populations were built up into large cities. But later
in the advance of Christian civilization, it became well understood that wealth did not bring
the best men on top,—that the species of talent
which rapidly accumulated money was not the
kind to be most enjoyed, nor to exert the best
influence in society, yet it was the kind to be
almost certainly thrown on top in large cities,
and thereby created bad standards for the aims
and ambitions of young men.

The advance of the race finally reached the
point where society demanded for its leaders
men distinguished for their intelligence, purity,
integrity, and disinterested usefulness,—qualities in the possession of which all could become rich who so desired, and no ambition
need be disappointed. Large cities did not
facilitate the accumulation of this kind of
wealth. It called for no intrigues or scheming.
It was not the kind of wealth which made one
poorer to enrich another. Converged capital
was not needed as its battle-ground. So those
who had the means left the cities from choice,
and those without means left from necessity,
and the leading schools of vice and crime were
closed for want of patrons. In this way the
large cities gradually disappeared from the face

of Mars, and the civilization of the planet was greatly advanced thereby.

In reading the literature of past ages on Mars, I found that matrimony had been a matter of extensive discussion, reaching through many generations. A great many theories had been advanced, thoroughly discussed, and then dropped out of sight, while others assumed, under examination, modified forms, and still exert controlling influence. The time was when young people contracted marriage with less thoughtful consideration than they would give to a business transaction involving only a few hundred dollars. They would dress their bodies so as to cover up all the defects and exhibit all the charms possible. They would do the same as to their minds and hearts,—would be careful to cloak their ignorance and all the faults of disposition and character, and bring to the front only those qualities of mind and soul which they believed would deceive and charm. This was the art of courtship, and the time was when it was practised as a fine art. Books and pamphlets were published instructing young people how to beguile and deceive the opposite sex, and thereby make matrimonial conquests. Mothers instructed their sons and daughters in the art, and rendered them all

possible aid in practising it. The sacred institution of matrimony, as well as all other good
things, was prostituted to the love of money.
Parents were anxious for their sons and daughters to marry riches at all events, whatever else
they might get or fail to get. The results of
marriage contracted under such circumstances
and influences can easily be imagined and need
not be described.

Young people often imagined they loved each
other when there was nothing akin to love between them. They liked each other's society,
and mistook this for love.

In an old book I found, in a chapter on
love, a definition that impressed me favorably,
reading as follows :

"Love is that relation between persons in
which the personality of the one is very nearly
lost in the other, in which each esteems the
other better than himself, and all selfishness
disappears. Liking is not loving. Admiration is not love, yet generally accompanies it.
Lust is not love, yet, in matrimonial engagements, it is too often mistaken for it. Love
must have a solid foundation in character. It
cannot build on outside appearances. There
can, therefore, be no such thing as 'love at first
sight.' Such love is mere fancy or lust, and
not at all akin to love. The object of it may

afterwards become the subject of real love, but is more likely to become the object of disgust when lust has been satisfied. A sympathetic nature is very liable to mistake pity for love. Love can spring up only from a thorough knowledge of character, and hearty approval of the inner workings of life and causes of action. A selfish nature is incapable of loving or being loved. The same may be said of an impure nature. Hence our methods of courtship and of matrimonial engagements are all wrong, and lead only to unhappiness. It is only by chance that parties occasionally happen to be properly and happily mated."

Later in the civilization of Mars, when the laws of heredity came to be well understood and properly appreciated by the more intelligent, parents strenuously objected to their sons and daughters marrying into families ignorant or unobservant of these laws. They were unwilling that their descendants should be tainted with the physical, mental, or moral diseases of those who had deliberately or negligently disregarded the higher laws of life.

When money ceased to give social rank and influence, one of the many incentives to improper marriages was removed, and conscience, justice, and good judgment began to exert sway in this class of contracts.

The present system of courting is quite a sensible admixture of business and sentiment, and interested me very much. If a gentleman desires to make the acquaintance of a lady with a view to a match, he addresses her with a request that she will make due inquiries and investigation as to his ancestry, his character, habits, disposition, etc., and asks the privilege of doing the same in relation to her, with a view to an ultimate contract of marriage, if, on better acquaintance, it shall be thought wise and best. If she declines this invitation, that ends the matter, and by both parties what has been said is considered strictly confidential. If she assents, then both parties go to work in earnest to ascertain the exact truth in relation to each other. In this investigation it is understood that the immediate friends of each may render all proper assistance. At the end of the investigation, if either party reports to the other that the result is unsatisfactory, the whole matter is at an end. But if both report satisfaction with the result, then the business portion of the courtship closes and the sentimental part begins. This is an honest, candid effort upon the part of each to ascertain whether their tastes, dispositions, and aims in life are such as readily to affiliate in such manner that each may supplement the other so that both may be made stronger and better fitted for the duties and proper enjoyments of life. If all is found well, reciprocal admiration and confidence become the basis of a true love, and they wed.

On Mars nearly all marry, and unhappy marriages are extremely few. Public opinion is such as to ostracize from society any person who will disregard the laws of heredity in selecting a life-companion. There is a fixed determination, almost universal, that disease and deformity of either body or mind shall not perpetuate themselves. The people believe in the survival of the fit only, and they encourage only the fittest. This makes another powerful motive to good conduct and the proper training and education of children, for none are willing that their descendants shall be ostracized from good society.

As stated elsewhere, the people of Mars are eminently religious, and they are a merry, cheerful, happy people. There is no infidelity, no atheism, no scoffing at religion there. All these things went out of existence when Dogmatic Theology went out. The various forms of disbelief grew up when Christianity was a creed, a code of doctrines,—when men were Christians if they believed as the doctors taught, and infidels if they did not. But, as the people increased in intelligence, they became dissatisfied with a religion of belief. They learned that devils believed and trembled, but were devils still. Believing did not necessarily make men any better. Such a religion did not meet human need, and was unsatisfactory. They felt that a true religion ought to improve a man's morals, while one consisting of assenting to certain doctrines did not necessarily do so, but it was certain to make infidels of all who dissented.

The most intelligent people, in and out of the church, therefore commenced mining down through the accumulated theological *débris* of past ages, in search of what man needed, and found it in the pristine, unadulterated teachings of Jesus of Nazareth. They found it in a form so clear and simple as to need no theological schools, no doctors of divinity, to make it understood by the most simple-minded. They found a religion which begins with "God be merciful to me a sinner," and proceeds in a pure life along the line of the Golden Rule, and universal love to mankind, and ends with life immortal. This religion met no rational opposition. All approved of penitence for wrong; all approved of one's doing as he would be done by; all approved of loving and doing good to all men; all approved of and desired eternal life: so there were none left to object or obstruct.

This simple religion is the religion of Mars, and has been for many centuries; and who will say it is not the religion of Jesus Christ,—pure Christianity? There men feel that they are glorifying God when they labor to perfect themselves and their race.

There, as here, they had an old catechism which asks the question, " What is the chief end of man?" The old answer of the theologians was, " To glorify God and enjoy him forever." They have also a more modern catechism, in which the same question is asked, but the answer is, " To perfect himself, and thereby glorify God and enjoy him forever." They think that Christianity teaches that man's heart must be cleansed and kept clean, and his moral and spiritual powers developed and made strong, so as to be a fit temple in which the spirit of God may abide, and thereby be enjoyed and glorified. It teaches that if the heart is right the life will be right,—that whether one eats, or drinks, or whatsoever he does, all will be to the glory of God. They believe that God is not glorified so much in words as in works.

Formerly, on Mars, there was a distinction between religious and secular employments. By the fictions of human conceptions, what was called the Christian world, in olden times, maintained a divorce between religion and the

18

common duties of every-day life. Mankind were occupied nearly all the time with eating and drinking, buying and selling, cheating and being cheated, making and losing, devising amusements and being amused, and with other and various business avocations. These things were called secular, and occupied fully nineteen-twentieths of all the waking hours, and many that should have been sleeping hours. During the other twentieth of the time, a part of the people devoted themselves to what they regarded as religious *duties*, which consisted mostly in listening to prayers, Scripture readings, music, and sermons. This curious mapping off of life into two distinct parts, denominated respectively secular and religious, was then the Christian civilization. Christianity was then embraced for its supposed efficacy in bridging the abyss between earth and heaven at time of death, but was ignored in the ordinary occupations of life. It was thought necessary to die by, but inconvenient and not needed to live by. But all these ideas have passed away. Now Christianity is the basis of all organizations, and is present supervising all the occupations of life. It permeates all business of all kinds, and goes and abides with men wherever they go. It supplies the balance-scale and the yardstick in all trading and trafficking among men. It inspires the employer with a sense of humanity and justice, and the employed with loyalty, integrity, and industry. It purifies the home, the school, and the workshop. It sweetens the amusements of adults and the sports of childhood. It enlivens and clarifies social circles. It warms the logic of the scientists, and adds spirit and life where before they could find only inert matter. It chastens literature, and adds melody to music. In brief, Christianity is immanent everywhere, all the time, and in everything. It knows no holidays: it has no special times, or seasons, or places. It is as much at home on the farm, in the parlor, the kitchen, the factory, the shop, the office, in the court-room, and the legislative hall, as in the church or cathedral. It controls men's actions on Saturdays and Mondays as much as on Sundays.

God hasten the time when such a Christianity, with such results, may cover the face of the earth !

THE END.

PRINTED BY J. B. LIPPINCOTT COMPANY, PHILADELPHIA.